TRINÀCRIA
A Tale Of Bourbon Sicily

ESSENTIAL PROSE SERIES 102

THE
ITALIAN CULTURAL FOUNDATION
AT CASA BELVEDERE

This book is made possible through the sponsorship of the
Italian Cultural Foundation at Casa Belvedere. Proceeds support
its ongoing mission "to preserve, promote and celebrate the rich
heritage of Italy by encouraging an appreciation of the Italian
language, arts, literature, history, fashion, cuisine and commerce
through educational programs, exhibits and events."

TRINÀCRIA
A Tale Of Bourbon Sicily

ANTHONY DI RENZO

GUERNICA

TORONTO • BUFFALO • BERKELEY • LANCASTER (U.K.)

2013

Photo: 19th century fresco from the Palazzo dei Normanni,
page 175, used by permission by Mark Sherouse.

Michael Mirolla, general editor
David Moratto, book designer
Guernica Editions Inc.
P.O. Box 76080, Abbey Market, Oakville, (ON), Canada L6M 3H5
2250 Military Road, Tonawanda, N.Y. 14150-6000 U.S.A.

Distributors:
University of Toronto Press Distribution,
5201 Dufferin Street, Toronto (ON), Canada M3H 5T8
Gazelle Book Services, White Cross Mills, High Town,
Lancaster LA1 4XS U.K.

First edition.
Printed in Canada.

Legal Deposit – Third Quarter
Library of Congress Catalog Card Number: 2013933968

Library and Archives Canada Cataloguing in Publication

Di Renzo, Anthony, 1960-
Trinacria : a tale of Bourbon Sicily / Anthony Di Renzo.

(Essential prose series ; 102)
Also issued in electronic format.
ISBN 978-1-55071-726-6

I. Title. II. Series: Essential prose series ; 102

PS3604.I27T74 2013   813'.6   C2013-901443-8

For
SHARON ELIZABETH

Beneath the shadiest cypress,
Within the coziest urn,
Is death any less cruel?
—Ugo Foscolo,
The Sepulchers (1807)

Contents

Catacombs of the Capuchins, Palermo.

PROLOGUE
The Latest Invasion

 PALERMO PREPARED FOR THE
latest invasion. The city was confident.
After twenty-five centuries of Romans
and Carthaginians, Normans and Arabs,
Spaniards and Britons, surely it could

handle a Hollywood film crew, even one led by a Milanese
duke. But at Punta Raisi, the welcoming committee faced
a more formidable (if less colorful) force than Garibaldi's
Red Shirts. Armed with a five-million-dollar budget,
Twentieth-Century Fox had assembled a battalion of two
hundred carpenters, ten dozen make-up artists, hairdress-
ers, and seamstresses, sixty cameramen, twenty electri-
cians, fifteen florists, and ten cooks. "If the Allies had
been this organized," joked the pug-faced mayor,
"Operation Husky would have been less a fiasco."

The studio publicist, a propaganda officer during the
war, laughed and pointed at the lanky figure on the
tarmac: "The Maestro's a better general."

A dying breed, the mayor conceded. According to the
studio press kits, which the publicist had distributed to
the delegation, the director descended from cardinals
and warlords, "whose massive red sarcophagi continue
to awe visitors to the Duomo di Milano." The Maestro,

the publicist said, never lost his dignity and never compromised his standards. "Gavin," he once explained, in his thickly accented English, "one must be in-*tran*-sigent." The publicist, an Illinois farm boy who had flunked out of Purdue, had learned the meaning of the word on their last film. When a fire broke out on the set, the Maestro had kept shooting until the ceiling collapsed. The producer berated him in the infirmary, but the duke — swathed in bandages like a B-movie mummy — merely pointed to his family crest: a blasted tower, copied from a fifteenth-century tarot deck, and the motto: *"Si fractus illabatur orbis, impavidum ferient ruinae."* If the world should shatter around him, the ruins would leave him undaunted.

The anecdote annoyed the city council. Where they expected to applaud this maniac's high-school Latin? The duke, fencing with the media, ignored the pursed lips. His crested hair gleaming with pomade, he seemed dressed for a duel. He wore a black silk shirt, white linen jacket, taupe slacks, and custom-made shoes.

"No," he said, "this story is not a paean to the past! At heart I'm a progressive, a humanist!"

The *paparazzi* hid their smirks. Like most aristocrats, the director voted left but lived right. Though an outspoken Communist, he had become a duke on his father's death, inherited his mother's cosmetics fortune, and owned five cars and a dozen houses. Liveried butlers at his Roman villa served pheasant on gold plate, while grooms stocked his four-hundred-year-old stables at Monza with stallions and gigolos. His Excellency rode both.

"But aren't studio epics risky in an age of television?" asked one reporter, a novice whose acne had become enflamed by the airport's heat and fumes. "The cost alone—"

The director's hawk-like face radiated contempt. Never contradict a man who called Maria Callas ... well, even the tabloids wouldn't print it. "Cost is meaningless!" he hissed. "Truth alone has value! The quest for authenticity knows no budget."

The mayor grunted. Geniuses can jaw about authenticity, but lesser mortals must deal with budgets. This film wasn't going to be another white elephant, was it? *Cleopatra*, he had read, already had cost Fox forty-four million and remained unfinished. But the publicist poured oil on these troubled waters. Epics were *very* marketable, he assured the mayor. Consider the largest grossing films of the past five years: *Ben-Hur*, *Spartacus*, *El Cid*, *Lawrence of Arabia*. Now Sicily would profit from its own epic, a sweeping tale about its marvelous past.

∽The past wasn't so marvelous, the mayor brooded. And Sicilians didn't need epics! They needed window fans and refrigerators! The only reason he had agreed to this crazy scheme was to stimulate tourism. Despite fanfare and expense, the Risorgimento centennial had flopped. Forced to gamble, the mayor was betting this re-enactment would do better.

Something had to be done. Palermo was bursting at the seams. Over the last decade, the population had risen by a hundred thousand. When a frantic Department of Public Works called for major construction, crooked contractors went into a feeding frenzy. The most prominent —a former cart driver who had hauled stone and sand in the slums—was connected to the Mafia. Thugs bribed or coerced officials to rubber-stamp over four thousand building licenses. Half the signatures were gullible pensioners, duped into applying for phantom benefits. To deflect scandal, the administration touted this house of cards, but critics called the boom the Sack of Palermo. Construction crews had destroyed the city's green belt and Art Nouveau villas and replaced them with shoddy apartment complexes. Meanwhile, the historical center, bombed during the war, still lay in ruins.

These conditions did not deter the director, whose scouts secured the best locations for his three-month shoot. He commandeered the Palazzo Gangi, with its gilded mirrors, Venetian chandeliers, and ceiling frescoes of rococo gods, for a ballroom scene. He converted a private chapel in the Cathedral of Palermo into a set. He uprooted telephone poles, repaved asphalt roads with cobblestone, and demolished an entire postwar neighborhood. At Ciminna, a mountaintop village thirty kilometers southeast of the city, he pillaged a three-thousand-year-old temple to Demeter to construct a marble mantelpiece for a fake palazzo.

A refuge was needed from the dust, din, and heat, so a decayed country manor in the suburb of Villabate, now the property of the University of Palermo's Department of Agriculture, was restored to its former glory and became the Maestro's private retreat. Here he tinkered with the script, browbeat designers, and auditioned extras.

A stream of local aristocrats flowed through his door. Their fine manners, better suited for a social at Circolo Bellini than a hastily improvised cattle call, could not disguise their discomfort. Some were scandalized because an American actor had been cast as a Sicilian prince. Others, who traced their ancestry back to Justinian, resented kissing the hand of this Northern upstart. But all competed fiercely for the chance to play their ancestors, however briefly: supernumeraries begging to become supernumeraries. The director pitied them. One *cavaliere*, a member of the Palermo Chamber of Commerce, wore a Rotary pin beside the Royal Order of the Two Sicilies. To meet real aristocrats, he must visit the Capuchin monastery.

∽The director traced the chiseled inscription:

> FUMMO COME VOI,
> SARETE COME NOI

We were like you, you will be like us.

Located on the western edge of the city, the Convento dei Cappuccini was famous for its extensive catacombs. Four centuries ago, the guide explained, the good monks discovered these vaults contained a mysterious preservative that could mummify the dead. Over time, eight

thousand Palermitani—from marchesas to maids—paid
handsomely to be buried here. To satisfy their patrons,
the enterprising monks perfected different preservative
techniques. During epidemics, they dipped bodies in arsenic or lime. They also invented new forms of em-
balming. But the most common method was dehydration.
Bodies were placed in cells, called strainers, which resembled a barbecue pit, and dried for about eight months;
then removed and washed in vinegar before being exposed
to fresh air. They were dressed and put in niches, coffins,
or on the walls, as instructed by the deceased or their
relatives. The oldest corpse, a tonsured ghoul, dated back
to the late sixteenth century. The youngest, a perfectly
preserved two-year-old girl, had died in 1920 and lay in
state in a special chapel. Nicknamed Sleeping Beauty, she
survived the Allied bombing in 1943 unscratched. Her
companions, the tourists discovered, were less fortunate.

Wandering the dank corridors, the director took notes.
Made of rough-cut stone, the exhibit halls were divided
into seven categories: Men, Women, Virgins, Children,
Priests, Monks, and Professionals. The corpses were
dressed in splendid but moth-eaten clothes and occupied
their own individual niches according to history and rank.
An assassin in a shredded doublet hung from the noose
that had dispatched him. A Bourbon colonel wore a
plumed cocked hat and a blue jacket with red piping and
cuffs. An American Vice Consul rested in his coffin with
a Mass card pinned to his frock coat.

According to the guide, the painter Velasquez also was buried here. The director doubted it, but Goya might have felt at home. Dangling from the limestone walls, elegant horrors wore top hats and tails, hoop skirts and bonnets. A clutch of doctors in dusty white coats consulted over a patient long past their aid. A series of mitered skeletons in gold vestments raised their bony hands in a blessing. Two eyeless tots in frayed Fauntleroy collars played catch with an invisible ball.

Without outside support, the guide continued, these mummies would crumble to dust. Fortunately, generous donations came even from overseas. Commendatore Attilio Tumeo, a Sicilian American businessman and philanthropist, whose maternal ancestors rested here, maintained this glassed crypt. The brass plaque read: "VALANGUERRA." Spaniards, thought the director. Judging from the 18th-century clothes, they must have come to Sicily with the Bourbons. A gentleman secretary wore a quill pen in a rotted ear. An amateur scientist held a pendulum and a tarnished pocket watch. A Carmelite nun knelt in prayer. A wooden rosary bound her wrists, probably to keep her fleshless hands from falling off.

But the most striking figure was a shrunken harpy, dressed in the late fashion of the *ancien régime*. She wore a moldering shawl, yellowed lace, and a cameo of Pallas Athena. Rubies glowed in her gorgon-headed walking stick, but her large wig was crooked. A beaded veil covered her ravaged face.

The director consulted his guidebook:

Zita Valanguerra Spinelli
(1794–1882)

Marchesa of Scalea, known as Trinàcria,
was a 19th-century literary figure and
caricaturist. A child prodigy, she captivated
the Queen of Naples during her brief exile in
Palermo. Widowed early, she ran a salon,
wrote epigrams, and entertained the court at
Caserta. When an indiscretion made her
unwelcome, she allied herself to the growing
Romantic movement. She promoted Bellini's
operas and supported the poet Leopardi,
until their rupture.

Practical and progressive, she cultivated
the friendship of the wine merchants
Benjamin Ingham and Joseph Whitaker, but a
failed lawsuit against her business partners
ruined her reputation and compelled her to
withdraw to her country estate at Villabate.
Embittered and reclusive, she became an
eccentric and wrote tracts against liberalism,
but her viciously funny political cartoons still
appeared in the popular journal *Don Pirlone*.

Spinelli's reactionary politics became
more rabid after Garibaldi's troops destroyed
her prized carriage. This outrage probably
contributed to a paralytic stroke. Confined to a

wheelchair and nursed by her granddaughter,
she spent her last twenty years writing,
translating Lichtenberg's aphorisms and
producing a monograph on Hume. Her
history of 18th-century Palermo, *Feste, Forche e
Farina* (*Festivals, Gallows, and Flour*) became a
source for Lord Harold Acton's two-volume
The Bourbons of Naples; but her erotic memoirs
remained unpublished until forty years after
her death. Her manor at Villabate, donated
to the University of Palermo, is still used
for special occasions.

My hostess, thought the director. He was about to bow,
but the small, imperious figure checked him. Rage had
frozen her expression into a silent shriek, which squelched
all flippancy. Even so, the director wondered if he should
incorporate her into his film, a bit of local color to set off
a scene. He gazed at the woman's clouded face, but his
attempt to pierce her veil failed. The beads were as numerous as flies on a windowpane. Only the empty sockets
were distinct. Their depth unnerved him. Lost in those
caves, he felt faint.

A draft blew through the catacombs, and somewhere
a door slammed. A chill prickled the director's skin, and
his ears buzzed. He could almost hear the mummies
whisper: *"You alone on earth are eternal, death ..."*

PART OF THE VILLA PALAGONIA'S
GALLERY OF ANCESTRAL BUSTS.

Chapter I
Eternal Death

YOU ALONE ON EARTH ARE eternal, Death. All things return to you. You cradle our naked being. In you, we rest secure — not happy, no, but safe from ancient sorrow. But why should that concern you happy children of this modern age? That warning at the gate does not apply to you. So you think. Much has changed since those words were carved, but one thing never changes: We all die, but still the mind clings to illusion until it rots. That is why we tell stories. To pretend otherwise, to rock ourselves to sleep and turn oblivion into a lullaby. Is it any wonder God never listens? Is it any wonder time unweaves every word?

We dead mock the living. And the more you chatter, the more we laugh. Our one consolation. Every joke is an epitaph for a feeling. It numbs regret and kills tedium. *La noia*, we call it. The cosmic boredom that is our common fate. And so we pass time listening to gossip. The Three-Twenty-Seven bus has become so bumpy. The pastries at Gulì's are so over-priced. The public works commissioner should be jailed. *Divertimenti* for an eternal salon.

These catacombs are cool and damp. Like the underground chambers in Bagheria, where we escaped the sirocco. Now we find refuge from life's heat. Muffled by stone, the traffic above us purls like a stream in a grotto. I would love to see these new machines, for father's sake. Made in Turin, I understand. More Piedmontese presumption. What do these Northerners know about carriages? They never parked at the Marina, in a car of ebony and gold, making love and eating jasmine-petal ices till two in the morning. They never defied Lord Bentinck's edict and drove through the Quattro Canti in a coach and six, the coins for the fine sown in the horses' plumed headbands and picked by the *carabinieri*. Ciccio, Regina's husband, did better work. But I cannot afford to be a snob. My great-grandson sells horseless carriages in America, and his money pays the rent and keeps me in style. The least he can do, considering he killed me.

Legally, I should not be here. Mummification was banned the year before I died, but the Villabatesi conspired on my behalf and confected ghost stories for the abbot. I prowled the fields at night in the shape of a she-wolf, they claimed. Dissolving into mist, I mingled with the oranges and lemons, turned into a poisonous cloud, and choked the field hands at dawn. I beat my former groom in his sleep. The old man could show his reverence the bruise from my crop. Somehow, they said, I must be appeased. My spirit would not rest, until I joined my ancestors. The abbot refused. The next morning, he awoke and found the saints knocked off their pedestals in the main chapel. He hastily obtained a dispensation and personally embalmed me.

Such stories shock the American tourists, but Sicily pampers and exalts her dead. On the Feast of All Souls, relatives come to offer us gifts and to change our clothes. Sometimes they reinforce our rotting limbs with wire hangers. A necessity, I'm afraid. Although we try to remain presentable, time and gravity can be cruel. Most of us miss a jaw, a hand, or a foot. Every time I see my reflection, I sigh. Did this scarecrow seduce at one ball the Princes of Salina, Assoro, Trabia, and Camastra? Penance for my sins. When I was young and glib, I angered Archbishop Pignatelli by calling the mummies *baccalá*, dried cod. Now look at me ...

∽ "You're still well preserved, Zita," Don Benjamin said. He took my blue-veined hand in his paw and kissed it. Charles II was right. Merchants are England's truest gentry.

I nearly forgot to be cross. "Does this flattery mean my order isn't ready?"

His nostrils flared slightly; otherwise, his face remained calm. In the security of his *baglio*, his dockside warehouse, Don Benjamin was imperturbable. Even after buying his title, Baron of Santa Rosalia, and mingling with the best of Palermitan society, the old Englishman still supervised his interests, here and in Marsala, and remained formidable behind a counter.

"On the contrary, Marchesa. We filled it immediately." He called: *"Picciotti!"*

Two aproned lads scurried to the back, and Don
Benjamin patted his belly. The *baglio* hummed like a bee-
hive. Hammers rang in the cooperage. Rolling barrels
rumbled. Clerks chirped over the accounts. So different
from my manor at Villabate, where only the cicadas
rattled. But Don Benjamin remained silent, the unmoved
mover, as serene as Aristotle's God. His bulk had increased
with his wealth. Fifty years ago, he was fit and trim. He
wore high collars and elegant cravats, and his auburn
hair was feathered in a Titus cut. Now he barely fit into
his swivel chair, and a button was missing from his serge
suit. His complexion had reddened, his nose broadened,
but he remained strangely virile. His musky cologne
penetrated the miasma of ripening *grillo*. Even so, I had
never forgiven him for siding with Don Joseph, who was
touring their vineyards in the Mazara Valley. My failed
lawsuit hung between us like a bad odor.

"Congratulations again," he offered, "on Regina's
confirmation."

"We were going to buy fireworks," I said, "but it seems
Garibaldi will provide them."

"Nonsense!" Don Benjamin grunted. "Young bloods
stirring up trouble, that's all."

Together, we had survived many upheavals, most recently the April riots, so we were indifferent towards the
rumor of another invasion. Nothing fundamentally would
change, except perhaps we would be forced to speak
Turinese instead of Neapolitan. Back then, Turin manufactured revolutions rather than carriages.

"We've played this lottery before," I said: "'20, '37, '48. All losing numbers. It's not entirely our fault. The game is rigged, God help us; but you've always known that, haven't you? That's why you prospered. You were never a gambling man, Don Benjamin."

"Not in politics, certainly; but trade is full of risks. Luck and pluck make profits."

"Then hide your cash box," I warned, "or the Red Shirts will confiscate it."

Jefferson Gardner entered, breathing fire. He was still youthful-looking, despite the mop of graying hair. His foster father, like other American sea captains, had come from Boston after the war with England and had settled in Marsala before prospering and moving to Palermo. Now Signor Gardner owned the captain's dry good stores along the Marina. He acted like an old salt himself. His manners were blunt, and he spoke Sicilian with a Boston accent.

"Look at this!" he sputtered, rattling a torn poster. "Some scamp pasted this outside!"

A cartoon showed a resplendent Garibaldi liberating a cemetery. He rode a white charger and wore a sash emblazoned with the words *"Fedele e Verace."* Overjoyed, the dead danced and scattered coins. The caption read: *"Anche i mercanti della terra piangono e gemono, perché nessuno compera più le loro merci."* And the merchants of the earth shall weep and mourn, for no man buyeth their goods any more.

"Socialist trash!" Signor Gardner said.

"I apologize for the iconography, gentlemen. Not in the best of taste."

"I don't understand," muttered Don Benjamin, his voice thicker than Yorkshire pudding. "The man was lionized in London. And what is he?"

"A gaucho," I said. "Poor Nelson wasn't deified until after his death."

"The admiral's morals were not always the most admirable." That was his great uncle, the famous Methodist, speaking. Don Benjamin attended the Anglican service at Palazzo Lampedusa every Sunday. Nevertheless, rumor accused him of wanting to be preserved in the Cappuccini. Perhaps he was following Jeremy Bentham's example.

"Then he should have stayed in Sicily. We like our heroes wicked. They make better tenors. But hawkers are notoriously tone-deaf. No English tradesman will accept an adulterous admiral with poor credit. What did Napoleon call you? A nation of shopkeepers" — and I unfurled a Cheshire grin. As the Romans said: *maior risus, acrior ensis*. The bigger the smile, the sharper the blade.

For the first time, Don Benjamin frowned. "True, Marchesa. But we beat Boney, didn't we, and everyone prospered; even our enemies. All we ask, in return, is a little gratitude."

A rebuke. Without shares in Ingham & Whitaker, I could not manage our estate. I resented the reminder but swallowed my bile. "Does Yankee Doodle agree?" I asked. "Can this commercial age afford to honor heroes?"

Signor Gardner pursed his lips and thought. "That depends, Marchesa," he said. "America certainly honors its heroes. But since their greatness depends on pleasing the people, they are always expendable. That is democracy."

An honest answer, if nothing else. "But that doesn't prevent you from boasting you're Paul Revere's grandson," I said. "Perhaps modern heroes need a trade. Signor Revere, I believe, was a silversmith who made false teeth." I tapped mine, for emphasis.

"Ha, ha, ha, ha!"

Olympian laughter. They were gods, after all, the English Croesus and his Yankee Mercury. The two controlled Sicily's most lucrative exports — wine, lemon, cotton — but most of their millions came from American investments, most notably New York transportation. We pretended to be friends again and discussed the company's holdings. I welcomed this chance to practice my English; but still, what a falling off! I, who had recited Pope for the King and Queen at the Palazzina Cinese, who had dined with the Hamiltons and entertained Coleridge, forced to parrot a prospectus. A huge map of New York State hung behind Don Benjamin's desk, highlighting the railroads and the Erie Canal, with the cities fat and brown as the figs ripening at our *masseria*. One was called Syracuse.

"Siracusa," I mused. "Does America plan to annex Sicily?"

"Not likely," Signor Gardner said.

"And yet she sends rifles to the revolutionaries. That will be bad for business, no?"

"Business survives everything, Marchesa. Even revolutionaries."

"Yes," I said. "Garibaldi didn't do well in *L'America*, I understand. Tried raising cash for the cause." This was twelve years ago, after the debacle in Rome. The New York papers had arranged a dockside welcome, supervised by that charlatan Barnum. The brass band came aboard, and the reporters found the General in his cabin, seasick and doubled over with rheumatism. They ignored his protests and hoisted him on their shoulders. Like a bale of goods. The General roared with pain, and the crowd cheered. Then came a gauntlet of civic groups and philanthropic societies. Then a month of superlatives in the press. Then ... nothing. "Death and fashion are sisters, gentlemen. The General spent the rest of his exile grinding sausages and shipping guano."

"Well," Signor Gardner said, "a little hard work never killed anyone."

Muffled thunder. The stockers had returned with six casks of wine. Don Benjamin ordered them brought to my carriage. "Now, Zita," he said, "I must insist. Half price."

"I don't need charity, signor," I said sharply.

"Please," he said soothingly. "Consider it Regina's confirmation present."

I relented and counted the money — one, two, three coral-pink notes — for the finest *stravecchio* on the island. As I left, Signor Gardner rolled up the poster and placed it in his desk.

"You're keeping Garibaldi? Why?" I asked.

"We'll use his face to sell vinegar," Gardner said. "You, of all people, should approve."

∽Poor Garibaldi. I hated that gaucho for wrecking my world, but he deserved better than to be turned into a condiment. What hero can survive in an age that does not distinguish the man on the horse from the man on the label? My great-grandson is one of the worst offenders.

When I last saw Attilio, he had become an old huckster. Accompanied by the mayor and six councilmen in ceremonial sashes, he touted his latest scheme. With enough investors, he boasted, he could open a factory near Tràpani and make horseless carriages. For promotion, he had designed a red racer named the Garibaldi, *"La Macchina dei Due Mondi."* I searched his face for some redeeming flicker of irony, but no, he was completely sincere. As Cagliostro the charlatan once told my father: "One must believe in miracles to convince others to believe in them. Success in this world depends on self-deception."

Attilio's slogans made the mayor and his entourage bob like sparrows at a feeder. Soon the whole flock cheeped. Words, words. The Sicilian vice. Honey puffs to fill the void. Myths, creeds, philosophies: all words.

Harmless when treated as a joke, fatal when taken as gospel. It wasn't enough for Empedocles to persuade himself he was a god; he needed to persuade others. So he threw himself down Etna, to disappear without a trace. He thought he had staged his apotheosis, but the volcano belched up a sandal and gave away the show.

When the cheeping stopped, Attilio crossed himself and knelt. Always such a devout boy. He alone kept me company in the conservatory, where I seldom spoke, unless to slur insults, but scribbled and cackled. He watched as my crablike hand scuttled across the pages of a morocco-bound notebook. At noon, he would wet my brow and temples with a damp cloth; at dusk, would wheel me to the window to smell the jasmine. He killed me with kindness. Sometimes, I stroked his cheek and called him *pronipuzzu*. More often, I rasped blasphemies. *God is an engine*, I said; *he turns and grinds us into dust.*

He still had his mother's winged eyebrows and high-bridged nose, but his cheeks were fuller, his mouth softer. So plump, so sleek, so smug: what would Regina have thought? Determined to make him a soldier, she forced him to drill in our courtyard. Naturally, he adored her, but she loved no one except the General. *La Garibaldina*: the same hysteric who had asked the midwife to kill her during labor and resented Ciccio for not shielding her from butcher bills. With such a corporal for a mother, the boy was bound to desert ...

∽"Pay attention, Tiluzzo!"

The rocking stopped, and the boy's eyes, which had wandered to the window, to the mimosas and the laundry drying in the courtyard, returned to be cradled by hers, to be rocked by her words no less than her body. He smiled bravely and wiped sugar crust from his mouth, his fingers sticky from honey puffs, and offered another to Regina, who only frowned and pressed his cheek between her tiny breasts and dandled him more sternly. Tiluzzo yelped. But she was deaf from inspiration, and I, three-quarters dead, condemned to watch and mock in silence, rolled my eyes and thought, *Maria, here we go again!*

And off they went, mother and child, rocking and rocking, Tiluzzo's eyes terrified, Regina's possessed. Her childlike frame quivered while her waxen face, youthful and ancient, merged again with that dream of glory. Faster and faster she rocked, her scar pulsing like a saber wound, and as the dust motes swirled in the sun-speared room and her tunic flared like a standard, we three no longer stifled in that hothouse parlor but galloped with Garibaldi over the plains of America.

We rode through the pampas and encountered wild stallions, with unshod hoofs white as ivory, their glossy backs shining in the sun, their tangled manes streaming behind them in the wind, and great black bulls charged through the short grass, but the General warded them off with a shot, and then the ostriches, half-running, half-flying, as they accompanied the guerillas, and the General laughed and cried: *"Reinforcements, boys!"* By the time they reached Montevideo, their blood was up (the heavy fighting had been exhilarating, not exhausting), so they shot out the street lamps and raided the warehouse for supplies.

"That's where they found the shirts!" said Regina. "Crates and crates of them, Tiluzzo. Just ordinary butchers' smocks destined for Argentine slaughterhouses. Dyed carmine to hide the bloodstains. But they were so handsome, Tiluzzo, so striking that they reminded the General of the scarlet gowns of the Saint-Simonians, the holy apostles of liberty. This is what they preached in his youth. Always remember these words, my son: *'The man who defends his own country or attacks another's is only a soldier. But the man who adopts another country as his own and offers it his sword and blood is a hero!'* And the General recognized those smocks as a sign from God and made them his official uniform. That's why his men were called Red Shirts, Tiluzzo, and why Garibaldi is called the Hero of Two Worlds."

She ran his hand over the tunic and said: "Do you feel its power? His strength passed into it, my son. Garibaldi himself gave me this shirt, and one day, I will give it to you."

"What nonsense are you telling him now?"

As usual, Ciccio had intruded his head in the parlor, grimacing and knitting his bushy black eyebrows. We feared and resented him, in part. That polished skull and handlebar moustache, those sarcastic eyes. His mouth, like an orc's in a marionette show, seemed to work on hinges. But Ciccio was the only one who could control Regina's fits, so we were grateful for him, too. He was our mastiff.

"Nothing that concerns you," Regina said, peering over her lozenge-shaped spectacles.

Ciccio snorted. "You stuff him with dreams and *sfinci*. No wonder he's as gluttonous as a priest — and as worthless!" He grabbed and slapped Tiluzzo's hand till the honey puff dropped.

Regina lifted the bawling child and carried him to the window seat. She preferred sitting there during their rows because the blinding light obliterated her surroundings. "If the nuns are kind enough to send him pastries," she said, "we should accept their charity."

"Of course," said Ciccio, "let him eat his way into Paradise. Honey puffs with custard, honey puffs with ricotta, honey puffs with marzipan. It's the Stations of the Cross in sugar."

"These are my great-grandmother's recipes," Regina reminded him. "She was abbess of that convent. I know that doesn't mean anything to you —"

"You're right: it doesn't. Little good it did her. Little good it does us."

"You want some?" asked the boy.

"Stop eating, priest!"

"I'm hungry!" whined Tiluzzo.

"Ciccio, don't yell! You know he's delicate."

"That soccer ball? If you dropped him off the roof, he would bounce."

"Not everyone's an animal," said Regina, and her face twisted with such hatred that even I shuddered. "This boy has a soul. That's why you hate him."

Ciccio barked a laugh. "What soul? The one you wove him? He wears that soul like you wear that rag!"

She pressed the boy's face against her as if she wanted to leave its imprint on her tunic. "Garibaldi gave me this shirt!" she said.

"*I* gave you that shirt!" roared Ciccio. "That crow shredded the one Garibaldi gave you, remember? I stuck up for you, and she beat me!" Then he wheeled on me and demanded: "True?" I grunted and barely nodded. "There! Papa said I'd live to regret it, and he was right!"

"In my heart," said Regina, "it is still Garibaldi's shirt."

"Tell your heart I have the receipt. I bought it from that American in the Foro Italico."

Signor Gardner had sold trunks of red shirts. They were in vogue after the Revolution. A factory in Paterson, New Jersey made them after Garibaldi took Sicily. Fashionable ladies wore them on Madison Avenue and Kew Gardens—to advertise their politics and win admirers. Would they have been as enthusiastic, if they had known the originals were butcher smocks? The advertisers never mentioned this. But it didn't matter because the American red shirts became more valuable. Made from the finest Indian silk, they fetched a high price in New York and London department stores, caused an international sensation at the Paris Exposition. More factories opened after that: Milan, Rheims, New Delhi,

Buenos Aires. Americans called the shirts garibaldis. Very popular with children. A tailor named Buttermilk sold patterns to Yankee mothers for fifty cents.

"Your Garibaldi comes from a counter," Ciccio sneered.

Regina covered Tiluzzo's ears. "You will not poison this boy! You stole my property and raped my body, but you won't corrupt my son!"

Ciccio placed a fist on his hip, clenching and unclenching it as if leisurely cracking walnuts. "My property, too. My family slaved for yours since the time they wore wigs: that makes it mine. I was your overseer and then your husband: that makes it mine, too. Keep your carcass! A beggar wouldn't touch it. But the boy belongs to me. My son: he's my son, too, you bitch, and all your stories won't change that! You're not the Madonna!"

"And you're not his father! Garibaldi is his father! And Garibaldi gave me this shirt!"

Ciccio smiled sarcastically. "Garibaldi gave Pino a red shirt, too. Tell Priest Face about my cousin Pino. He wore a red shirt when he fought the landlords, but your darling Garibaldi had him shot. I was at the execution. They stood him against a wall, confused as a kid. Then the firing squad came, all Red Shirts, and the poor idiot smiled. He clapped and whistled and pointed to his red shirt, then he pointed at theirs and waved. They just stared like statues, knelt, and fired. Pino was surprised. Not me."

"You are a horrible man."

"And you," he said, "are a poet."

True. All poets are cruel, even the gentlest, as I
discovered in Naples ...

∞ "You have wonderful manners, Marchesa," Leopardi
said, "but you aren't civilized." His melancholy face was
paler than the pillow propping his head, but his cobalt
eyes glinted with malice.

The insolence! My smile hid my rage. I had not traveled
all the way to Villa Ferrigni to be insulted by a sick child!
Sarita, his publisher, had promised me this interview for
my forty-second birthday, but had failed to warn me that
the poet was a querulous eccentric. Ranieri, his friend
and nurse, endured his tantrums. Perhaps I should have
remained an anonymous patron. Well, too late now. I
held my smile and glanced out the window.

The villa was located near Mount Vesuvius, between
Torre del Greco and Torre Annunziata. A Palladian
retreat, its pink façade displayed a rather plain sundial
with the motto: *"Sine Sole Sileo."* Without the sun, I am
silent. The original owner, Canon Giuseppe Simioli, had
installed a seismograph in the study, a necessary precaution
because of the volcano. Leopardi, a connoisseur of
catastrophe, delighted in it. From the window, I could
see the distant ruins and barren plains. Broom trees dotted
the slopes of Vesuvius. The breeze carried their scent but
gave no relief. All I could think about was wounding that
little hunchback! With part of my donation, he had
engraved and circulated a squib about me at Caffé d'Italia:

"TRINÀCRIA the scholar, in Ovid delves.
Her books and her lovers she marks and shelves."

I turned to him and assumed a bantering tone. "And you, Contino, are a fraud," I said, and tapped the book I had brought for him to autograph. He knew I was baiting him, the mooncalf, but was still curious. Writers are so vain.

"A fraud, Marchesa?"

"Yes," I said, "in your poems and essays. That's why I came to visit. That's what fascinates me about your work: its sheer duplicity. You know that truth, love, and honor are illusions, but you believe in them anyway. What's worse, you make others believe in them, even as you warn against them. Hypocrisy, don't you think?"

Leopardi laughed. It was a strange laugh, bleak but hearty, and he subdued it to prevent himself from coughing up more blood.

"What's so funny?" I snapped. "I practically call you a pimp and you laugh?!"

"Excuse me, Marchesa. But I've never been accused before of being a believer. Manzoni would be amused." He stifled a chuckle.

Croak, toad. I will squash you yet.

"Do you mock me?" I said.

"No, of course not." And he groped for and patted my hand, still smooth thanks to aloe lotions but beginning to vein. "I'm such a brat. Ask poor Ranieri, who must endure my nerves."

Ranieri, patient and solid as an ox, smoothed the covers and removed the tray. "He's a big baby," he said mildly, patting the invalid's cheek. "He bawls for ices."

Pain checked Leopardi's laughter. "You see? Forgive me!" he implored. "The old should always forgive the young."

What a strange little man! Not at all what I had expected. I had imagined Prince Hamlet and instead found a bedridden, half-blind hunchback with the face of a homely choirboy. Was *this* the voice of unrequited love? I mocked myself for being seduced by his poems and pretended to prefer his mordant dialogues. My favorite was "Friedrich Ruysch and His Mummies," perhaps because Papà had kept anatomical books in my nursery.

"I've never forgiven the young," I said. "Even when I was young myself."

"Then you don't believe in happiness," he said with a sigh.

"I don't believe in foolishness," I retorted.

"And how do you define foolishness?"

Pretending life is something it isn't. But I had learned that truth too early. When I was six, my mother went mad because my father had taken yet another mistress, and I concluded that love is a trap for the blind. Papà scoffed at love. A gigantic twitch. Galvani had proved that to his satisfaction. Women's legs just happen to be shapelier than frogs. Watch! He chuckled over a pickled specimen, operated a battery, and jolted its thigh. When he pricked a finger on a brass hook, he fed the blood to his praying mantis Alecto. I didn't need Monsieur Voltaire to tell me the world is a watch that's been abandoned by its watchmaker. My father taught me that when he lost his soul to his inventions. But what business was that of Leopardi's?

"Foolishness, Contino, is clinging to childhood when one should be an adult. I always hated toys. I had more practical pastimes."

While the other girls complained about the cost of trinkets, ribbons, and dolls, I memorized the price of crops, wines, and vegetables. Let them worry their beads and pray for husbands. I had at my fingertips the weights and measures of solids, liquids, and money. I knew how many *tumoli* made up a heap of grain or soil; how many *rottoli* and how many *coppi* formed a barrel of olive oil or a cask of Marsala; how many *tarì*, how many *carlini*, how many *griani* went into an *onza*. Above all, how many *salma* divided our land.

By the time I was fourteen, I was managing the farm. Don Alfonso's interest was purely theoretical, even when improving the drainage. Why did the water in our suction pumps never rise farther than five *canne*? Atmospheric pressure! To counter-balance it, Papà built an elaborate vacuum device, based on seventeenth-century German design. The water failed to rise even an inch, far less five *canne*. After blaming the workers, for supposedly disregarding his instructions, Papà consoled himself by writing a paper on Torricelli for the Royal Society.

"Now do you understand why I hated the laughter of my playmates?" I said. "It was rooted in ignorance. I detested their daydreams and make-believe games."

"But you envied them, too, no?"

My jaw dropped, and Leopardi laughed.

Even then, I was practicing for now. *Quite chapfallen, darling?* I ask my reflection. *Not one tooth left to mock your own grinning?* My playmates at Bagheria often ran home, howling, with bleeding noses and ears. Of course, I envied them! I envied their innocence, just as I envied Leopardi's genius, Don Benjamin's drive, and Regina's courage. I even envy the sheer banality of the living.

MEMORIAL STATUE OF PALLAS ATHENA
IN THE GARDENS OF VILLA PALAGONIA.
ATHENA IS DONNA ZITA'S GUARDIAN AND PATRON.

Chapter II
Family Pride

IMMORTALITY IS A BORE. ENDLESS night darkens laborious thought in the uncertain mind; the dried-up spirit feels its drive to hope and desire gutter out; and so, freed from trouble and anxiety, we endure the grinding, vacant ages unwearied. Our one pastime is tracing our pedigree.

Such pride must seem ridiculous. All genealogies consist of guesses and embellishments. What lineage can we possibly trace, when life itself is written in water? But in my day, families fell into four distinct categories: those who from humble beginnings slowly attained surpassing greatness; those who from exalted beginnings maintained and upheld their original glory; those, like us, who declined from greatness into obscurity, just as a pyramid tapers from a massive base to an insignificant point; and those — the most numerous — who had neither an illustrious beginning nor a remarkable mid-course and so perished nameless. Today, only the last kind of family exists, which is why greed and spite have conquered the earth.

Before I was tanned, stuffed, and placed in this niche, I wrote our family's history, but Regina burned the

manuscript. For her, history began and ended with
Garibaldi. "Why chronicle a century and a half of
stupidity?" she asked. Poor fool. Didn't she realize we
can no more change our ancestors than choose our
posterity? I scribbled my reply: *"Because nothing conveys a
greater sense of the infinite than stupidity."*

∞My grandfather, Don Miguel Valanguerra de
Salamanca, landed in Palermo on July 10, 1735, a week
after Charles I's coronation. A bankrupt hidalgo, he carried a damaged escutcheon, a gilt-edged reference, and
a first edition of the *Quixote*. This last item proved the
most fitting. Like Sancho, Grandpapa dreamt of ruling
a mythical island, but incompetence prevented him from
becoming little more than the Under Secretary to the
Lieutenant Governor. Solitary and eccentric, he married
late, establishing a pattern for the males in our family,
and remained a sallow-faced clerk, courtly but shabby,
with a wispy Vandyke and a collection of quill pens. He
wasted his life composing a tome on Cervantes, which
contains this odd but revealing line: *"A knight errant thrives
on errors and errands."*

But his son, Don Alfonso, sparkled with brilliance.
After studying commerce and mechanics with Antonio
Genovesi in Naples, my father served first as a military
engineer, then as an army treasurer. Papà had a face like
a sundial's, and his tight-fitting uniform accentuated a
proud but stiff carriage. Distinction in the field led to his
appointment as Ambassador to Malta. As a reward for

securing a lucrative trade agreement with Turkey, King
Charles made him Baron of Campofiorito di Catena, a
recently forfeited title, and awarded him an estate at
Bagheria. He never became a major landlord, however,
considering property "a Physiocratic fetish." Instead, he
retired early, married the younger daughter of the wealthy
Commendatore Branciforte, and dedicated himself to
scientific pursuits. He experimented with physics, cor-
responded with Gianbattista Beccaria on steam and elec-
tricity, and lectured on time and motion at the University
of Palermo. His two hobbies were clocks and women
because both needed winding.

Flagrant disregard for his baptismal and marital vows
compelled my mother, the pious Donna Elvira, to spend
most of her time praying in the chapel and championing
the canonization of local saints. When she bore a daughter, Mamma was convinced God had vindicated her, but
I was destined to become a greater skeptic than Papà.
Originally, he had wanted to name me Zisa, after the
Norman-Moorish pavilion outside Palermo, a masterpiece
of geometry, but Mamma overruled him at my baptism.
Her child would have a Christian name, she insisted, so
I was baptized Zita, after the Spanish oratory in Palermo
honoring the Battle of Lepanto. I came to loathe my name.
In Sicilian, *zita* means fiancée, and even as a child, I de-
tested the thought of being plighted to anyone. Besides,
the only St. Zita in the calendar is that simpleton from
Lucca, the patron of servants. My motto always has been:
"Non serviam." For my first name day, Mamma gave me

a wooden duster. Supposedly, I flew into a rage and plucked every feather.

Henceforth, the Baron possessed me. He taught me the laws of physics rather than the Ten Commandments. Isolated in his study, I rolled iron balls down an inclined plane and timed their acceleration. When I was three, I accompanied him to the Ucciardone, where he supervised the construction of drop scaffolds of his own design. "God will not punish you," I lisped to one condemned prisoner. "Gravity will." My distraught mother begged me to learn compassion and forced me to read an illustrated life of St. Francis, but Don Alonso outfoxed her again. He removed the book cover and attached it to a collection of prints by the Dutch anatomist Friedrich Ruysch, every bit as gruesome and baroque as the mummies in the Cappuccini.

Ruysch had assembled a dozen allegorical tableaux of baby skeletons against backgrounds of body parts. There were geological landscapes of gallstones and kidney stones, botanical gardens of injected and hardened veins and arteries for trees, petrified alveoli and capillaries for bushes and grass. The tiny skeletons were ornamented with symbols of mortality. Hands held mayflies, which live but a single day. Skulls wept into handkerchiefs woven from pleated meninges. Snakes and worms, made of writhing intestines, wound around pelvises and rib cages.

When Donna Elvira caught me perusing these abortions, she gasped and shook me. "Have you no soul?" she cried. "Have you no soul?" She sank to the floor and wept.

I should have comforted her, I suppose, but Ruysch had made me pitiless. Gazing at her face, I saw only a blubbering skull. I pointed and giggled. Mamma cringed and crawled backwards. Alarmed by the uproar, Don Alfonso burst into the room and saw his wife behaving like a wounded crab. His shoulders flapped from chuckling, and he scooped me up and held me against his hip. We both pointed and laughed until the tears rolled down our cheeks. Mamma composed herself, rose, and left the room. Her skirts swished as she closed the door behind her.

Defeated, Donna Elvira petitioned the Archbishop to take the veil and became Mother Superior of the Convent of the Holy Trinity at Petralia Sotanna. A tireless administrator, a master baker and, by popular repute, a saint, she was adored by the nuns, despised by her husband, who intercepted and destroyed her letters to me. Not that I cared. I had lost all respect for her. But one Easter she smuggled a note in a box of *cannoli*. "Serving others," she wrote, "sweetens life's bitterness." I tore and returned it with the untouched *cannoli*, and never heard from her again. She died two years later on July 15, 1807 (allegedly in an odor of sanctity) during the festival of Santa Rosalia and was placed in the Cappuccini. She left me five hundred hectares of prime land below Cozzo Cannita, cultivated a century earlier by the Abbé Antonio Agnello, Sicily's greatest botanist and the founder of Villabate. This bequest pleased me, for I was fiercely attached to the Conca d'Oro, the honey-colored plain surrounding Palermo.

"I don't believe in God," I told my father, "but I believe in those hills."

This comment baffled Don Alfonso, a true disciple of Galiani, who thought land had no economic value in and of itself. But he never despaired of my intelligence. By the time I was twelve, I had started calculus and could speak French and English. At Villa Urania, our Bagheria estate, I entertained visitors. Among them was Samuel Taylor Coleridge, then secretary to the Governor of Malta, who gave me a copy of *Lyrical Ballads*. As an antidote, the Baron advised me to read Bacon and Hume, but cautioned against discussing such things too freely.

∞King Ferdinand and Queen Maria Carolina hated new ideas. After transplanting their court to Palermo to escape the French, they equated intelligence with treason. "Every bookworm is a Jacobin!" the Queen would growl, thirsting to avenge her guillotined sister Marie Antoinette. We were introduced at the Chinese Pavilion when I was five. I had narrated "The Triumph of Science," a masque organized by the English ambassador, Sir William Hamilton, to display my father's inventions. Pleased with my performance, the Queen awarded me a cameo of Minerva, worth five hundred *tarì*. Sir William, an avid collector, had found this treasure at a small shop in Torre del Greco. Pinning the brooch on my bodice, Maria Carolina cupped and lifted my chin.

When our eyes met, I flinched, for I hated being touched. My cheeks burned, and the Hapsburg jaw hardened into granite. "As proud as she is accomplished. Good!" The Queen grimly smiled. "We must find her somebody special."

As I grew into a young woman, I often came to court and became the Queen's favorite. Fine-boned and angular, I was striking rather than beautiful. Saucy eyes and sensual lips compensated for my aquiline nose and lantern jaw. Empire gowns showed off my exquisite shoulders and lime-shaped breasts. With a voice pitched like a clarinet, I was a virtuoso of impertinence. Everyone encouraged me, and I was too dazzled by the attention to notice the Queen eye me like Alecto, Papà's pet praying mantis. Then the ax fell. When I turned sixteen, Her Majesty engaged me to Vitello Spinelli, the rich but obscenely fat Marchese of Scalea. I wept and appealed to my father, who shrugged and peered through his brass telescope.

Love works wonders, he said, but money makes marriage. Without this alliance, he could not afford to continue his research. Surely, I did not want him to sacrifice his life's work, did I? Marriage is a mere contrivance, spouses as interchangeable as piston rods. But that fact needn't curtail one's freedom, as his own example proved. Domestic bliss requires indifference. For a woman, the best way to cultivate the necessary detachment is studying the ridiculous faces a husband makes on her wedding night. That, at least, was Da Vinci's advice.

On our honeymoon, Vitello shattered my thighbone and permanently lamed me. I returned to Bagheria. When Don Alfonso saw me walking with a cane, he bit his

palms, not consumed by guilt so much as pride. That
lout had crippled his daughter. *His* daughter! Regaining
his calm, he submitted two facts: a son would strengthen
my position among the Spinellis, whatever happened to
my husband; Vitello loved almonds.

"Make the most of this information," he said.

At first, his words puzzled me. Almonds enflame desire, encourage conception, and enhance pregnancy.
Should I orchestrate a tryst to secure an heir? Then I
remembered that arsenic smells and tastes like almonds.
I smiled, kissed Papà good bye, and reunited with Vitello.
Mamma would have been pleased. We lived together for
a year, until I had Alvarito. Then I poisoned my husband—very frugally, I'm pleased to say. Why waste money
on Aqua Tofana when a simple cosmetic will do?

Like most court ladies, I used arsenic oxide to whiten
my face and to treat pimples. I stole from my childbed,
slipped into the kitchen, mixed the powder with sugar,
and sprinkled it on a fig and almond cake. The next morning the maid served Vitello the cake at breakfast. I might
have repented, if his death spasms had not resembled his
lovemaking. My in-laws suspected something, but the
heat prevented an autopsy and the Queen squelched further investigation. To put the best face on things, she
agreed to become Alvarito's godmother.

༄After the funeral, Papà and I reconciled. He swore to
make amends. Next time I could marry whomever I
pleased. My eyes fell on Benjamin Ingham, the young

wine merchant, who had come to Palermo to challenge the monopoly of old John Woodhouse, the British fleet's chief supplier of sherry and Madeira. Despite the American War, Ingham had raised enough capital to start his own business and to build a *baglio*. He supervised the construction himself, unashamed to go shirtless among the workmen. He also invested in shipping, waiting for the inevitable day when the blockade would end and Sicily once again could send its oranges and lemons to New York and Boston. As a pretext for meeting him, I brought him our citrus from Villabate.

A Yorkshireman, Signor Ingham spoke as if he were chewing roasted pumpkin seeds. But his eyes sparkled with intelligence, and his jaw was firm and manly. A thick neck and large collarbone foretold future girth, but for now, he was slender and energetic. His broad hands molded the air when he talked. Although he lacked formal education, he was a voracious reader and could converse on many subjects. True, he had an ugly temper, but he reserved it for bores, humbugs, and procrastinators. With decent people, whatever their rank, he was kind and charming. Even so, he was lonely. After twice being jilted by flighty society girls, he confined himself to his warehouse. If I wanted to win him, I must proceed slowly.

At first, we limited ourselves to conducting business and discussing politics. Eventually, we attended social functions and took coffee at my salon. He enjoyed my company, he declared, because I was the only woman he knew who spoke as bluntly as a man. For an Englishman, this was practically a marriage proposal. The time had come to invite him to Bagheria.

Don Alfonso seemed pleased. A passionate Anglophile, he recalled how he had delivered a paper at the Royal Society and had observed the London stock exchange. As we sipped Signor Ingham's Marsala on our terrace, tiny glasses of gold, amber, and ruby nectar, Papà became more expansive. He favored an English constitution for Sicily and predicted trade between our two islands would eradicate poverty. But these progressive ideas did not extend to his daughter, no matter how much he enjoyed Signor Ingham's wares. "If I may make an analogy," he offered. "A captain may marvel at a chronometer and appreciate its benefits to navigation, but he does not mistake this device for a first mate, much less a son-in-law."

He drained his glass, bowed, and retired. Signor Ingham also made his excuses and left. The following week he sent me a blistering letter and ended our friendship. Later he kept company with Alessandra Spadafora, the Duchess of Santa Rosalia, who became his mistress.

To avenge myself, I also courted shame. I opened a salon and collected lovers as eagerly as I collected titles. I wrote squibs, signed Trinàcria, and chose a bellicose motto from Book VII of the *Aeneid*: "*Proelia virgo dura pati cursuque pedum praevertere ventos.*" The virago Camilla, though only a girl, "hardily bears the fray and fleetly outruns the wind." These words adorned a crest I had designed: a greyhound in a studded collar leaping over a triskelion. The three-legged hex sign symbolized not only Sicily but also me. I was three-legged, too, but had traded my cane for a gorgon-headed walking stick. The ruby eyes intimidated some wooers, but most young men risked everything to ride in my ebony and ivory coach. On moon-less nights, I parked on the docks and rutted until the city watch intervened.

I was no less brazen in broad daylight. Defying the British governor, I drove through the Quattro Canti, the crowded heart of the old capital, and menaced pedes-trians. When Lord Bentinck impounded my carriage, I vowed to seduce him. Madame de Staël was all the rage, so I appeared before him in a scarlet dress and a turban trimmed with peacock feathers. "I am Corinna," I lisped, "and you are Lord Oswald." Bentinck suggested that I buy a harp, escorted me from his office, and kissed my hand. *"Molto galante,"* I said, "but still a declaration of war."

I set up camp in Piazza Pretoria and slept in a silk tent. Every morning, I washed my hair in the Fountain of Shame, a stone orgy bequeathed to Palermo by Viceroy Pedro de Toledo from a second-rate Tuscan villa. I break-fasted on pomegranates, read *Corinne,* and awaited Bentinck. Imitating the statues in the fountain, I grimaced, bared my teeth, and stuck out my tongue. The governor ignored me for a week, until I blocked the entrance to Palazzo Pretorio and denounced him pointblank. Pointing to the Genius of Palermo, the city emblem guarding the staircase, I called the Englishman a serpent at our breast. *"Panormus,"* I cried, *"conca aurea suos devorat alienos nutrit!"* Palermo, the golden dell, devours her own and feeds foreigners.

When I began drawing a crowd, Lord Bentinck surrendered. *"La Bestia Feroce,"* the Ferocious Beast, who had muzzled the Queen of Naples and had banned sorbet from the Sicilian parliament until it approved his constitution, was no match for a twenty-year-old bluestocking. The governor returned my carriage and tolerated my future indiscretions. The greatest outrage was my affair with Salvatore Gravina, the Prince of Palagonia, who had married and grown tired of his young niece. At the Villa dei Mostri, his palace at Bagheria, we paraded nude in endless halls of glass. The guests were shocked.

"Mirror yourselves in these walls," I invited, "and reflect on human folly!"

The scandal killed Don Alfonso. The servants found his body in the laboratory. Stricken, he had collapsed on the terrarium. Glass encrusted his hands and cheeks, and the pet mantis, Alecto's great-granddaughter, lapped his bleeding ear. For convenience, the funeral was held at Anime Sante, but he had willed his body to be preserved at the Cappuccini; an odd request for a man who had memorized Lucretius and had looked forward to the dissolution of his atoms.

"My soul," he had announced cheerfully, "will melt like boiled chocolate!"

This gave me an excuse not to mourn. During the service, I remained dry-eyed and bemused, but Alvarito became hysterical. *"Nonno!"* he sobbed. *"Nonno, nonno!"* Humiliated, I dragged him from church and cuffed him.

"Get used to it," I said. "Everything abandons you in the end, except land."

✺ "We lost five more lime trees," Ciccio reported.

Regina glared over her gold spectacles. Any mention of practical matters deepened her crow's-feet. "What's that to me?" she said flatly. "As you've boasted often enough, this is your land now. Not mine."

Ciccio looked flustered. "Thought you'd want to know, that's all."

"I don't," she said and resumed playing with Attilio. Tin Bourbons and tin Red Shirts littered the floor, and Tiluzzo wore a bandage over an imaginary head wound. When Regina and Ciccio had been playmates, her infatuation with Garibaldi had amused him. Even as a boy, he was cynical and pear-shaped, but he had tolerated her peculiarities because she was brave. Now she was spiteful and ungrateful.

"Another campaign?" he said. "If it weren't for me, you wouldn't have these toys!"

She ignored him. He bit his knuckle and glanced at me. His expression became crafty. When sarcasm fails, there is always solicitude.

"Cara," you've not eaten in two days. Wouldn't you like some cardoons? An army must travel on its stomach, after all. Isn't that right, Grandma?"

A chuckle gurgled in my throat, until Regina scowled at me.

"Back to the dirt where you belong!" she told Ciccio. "Who digs the soil, digs his grave!"

This was unjust. Although born a peasant and briefly replacing his father as overseer, Ciccio had become a successful carriage maker. Borrowing cash, he converted our stables into a workshop. His squat fingers looked bloodstained from an addiction to red pistachios, but they worked wonders with gilt and ebony, glass and upholstery. His specialty was painting faux coats of arms on middle-class broughams. Even so, aristocrats offered their custom. Having lost their coaches in the revolution, they were obliged to lease new ones. For a little extra, Ciccio would substitute his plain doors with decorative ones salvaged from destroyed or confiscated vehicles. The gentry had taken every measure to save face. Some bribed the Red Shirts. One countess slept with an entire regiment. Another hid her door behind a triptych by Messina. Such pride may be admirable, but it cannot support an estate. Without Ciccio's income, we would have starved.

After my stroke, the *masseria* languished. Don Joseph, no longer opposed by Don Benjamin, had cancelled my contract with the firm, and no one else in the family had the brains or the money to manage our affairs. Desperate, the clan enticed Ciccio to marry Regina. It should have been a solid marriage of convenience. Instead, the carriage business barely covered rising property taxes, while Regina's pedigree scarcely legitimized Ciccio's new status. The farm hands called him "Don" to his face and laughed behind his back.

Ciccio played the son of the soil, even as he cultivated bourgeois tastes and habits. He bought onyx cuff links for his silk shirts, which he kept in a lacquered box on his dresser, but still affected the dress and manner of a country *padrone* before his men. In the fields and workshop, he wore an open-necked white shirt, a gold earring, black pants, and a red bandana. He waxed his moustaches and even daubed his bald head with olive oil so that it gleamed like a billiard ball. Regina considered him a brute and a poseur and barricaded herself in the conservatory, sheathed in a red tunic, and pounded marches on an out-of-tune spinet. Ciccio retaliated through fornication, preferring Palermo's genteel brothels to our own town whores.

Marriage, Papà once joked, is "a tiny Algiers" consisting of a bey, a mistress, two slaves, one eunuch, one cook, one guard, and one torturer; total population: two. That certainly was true at our home. When the royal couple was not impaling each other, the sultana would withdraw to her private seraglio with the crowned prince and the dowager. Tiluzzo and I were her prisoners. To pass the time, the boy parroted Leopardi.

"O Italia! I see our ancestors' walls and arches, columns, effigies and towers —"

But not their glory. If he stumbled over a phrase, his mother sighed like a martyr and made him repeat the entire passage. Fine recreation for a two-year-old! Still chubby, Tiluzzo had grown solemn and careworn. Dark circles ringed his eyes, and boredom made him languid.

Only his hands were lively, forever taking apart broken watches and music boxes. Regina, meanwhile, plunked songs of yearning on the spinet: *"Ahhhhh, patria mia! Mai più ti rivedrò!"* Neither noticed if a gecko crawled up my paralyzed leg or a fly brushed my lip.

∾Torpor and sorrow marked our days. The relentless heat, the droning cicadas, the sluggish meals and interminable siestas, the suffocating smell of rotting bougainvillea, Regina's mournful voice forever keening: these made life a mirage. To break the monotony and isolation, we took long carriage trips. Usually, these were limited to the cathedral at Monreale or the Greek ruins at Segesta; but if Regina needed further escape, we would tour the eastern part of the island, journeying through palm, acacia, and broom, then hugging the coast and marking the cities along our route: Cefalù, Patti, Messina, Taormina, Catania, Siracusa, Modica, Ragusa, Gela, Agrigento. But however far or fast we traveled, we never shook a sense of futility and stasis. Round and round and round we went, three mules grinding corn.

During the hottest months, we stayed in the remains of Villa Urania. Ivy overgrew the concave-shaped façade, the double staircase was cracked, and rust had sealed the bronze dome of the observatory. But the park remained pleasant, if ill-kept, and the terrace still commanded a stunning view of the sea. I almost accepted the fact that the square had been renamed Piazza Garibaldi. As Regina treated a migraine in the underground chambers, Attilio wheeled my carcass around Bagheria. Villa Palagonia was just down the Corso Umberto. I've always treasured the scenes of my infamy. Treasure yours. We all have skeletons in the closet. If they must rattle, they may as well dance.

Tiluzzo and I wandered for hours amid topiaries and grotesque statues. The crooked palms and twisted cacti, the ceramic hunchbacks and tufa satyrs dizzied the boy, who gripped a parasol to shield me from the sun. Don Salvatore's half-brother, the hunchbacked and scrawny Prince Ferdinando, created these monsters. Twisted in both mind and body, he was a notorious cuckold. Because his wife flaunted her numerous infidelities, he ordered artisans to sculpt frightening caricatures of her lovers as clowns and drunks, freaks and beggars, cripples and dwarfs. The princess and her male harem cringed, but their shame deepened when Don Ferdinando charged public admission. After he died, Don Salvatore added but one more monster to the collection: a bare-breasted and leering gorgon with my face. Carved on its marble base was the name TRINÀCRIA.

When we found the statue, I began to snicker. Without understanding, Tiluzzo joined me. But my laughter grew and grew until I gagged. The coughs and whoops alarmed Tiluzzo, who dashed for help. Squinting in the sun, cheeks streaked with tears, I howled at my stone reflection.

∽ "We're all monsters," I explained. "Only some of us are unashamed."

Leopardi considered this point. "Then we indeed are made in God's image."

"Or nature's," I said.

"It makes no difference. Both are cruel step-parents who punish us for no reason."

He was alluding to his deformity, a tautology as well as an affliction. The universe is unjust because I am a hunchback; I am a hunchback because the universe is unjust.

"Then doesn't that give us the right to be cruel? Why pity mankind if life is so pitiless?"

"Precisely because it is pitiless we must pity mankind," he replied.

"Circular reasoning, *carinu*. Does that pity extend to those who are cruel to us?"

"Socrates would have said so."

He had practiced this philosophy, Ranieri confided, distributing candy to the urchins in his hometown who had pelted him with snowballs. How dare they call him *gobo*, he teased. Now he would revenge himself. Here were *his* snowballs! And from his pocket he fished and distributed a handful of round white sweets.

"You must take hemlock, rather than bitters, with your coffee," I remarked.

He smiled bleakly. "You and I have drunk from the same cup, Marchesa."

"And what would that be?" I joked. "The Pierian spring?"

"Family pride," he said, "the fountainhead of cruelty."

He spoke from experience, having been born into the noblest family in the most ignoble province in Italy. For five centuries, the Leopardi had been a name in the Marches, an illustrious procession of magistrates, priors, bishops, canons, and knights of Malta. When the Madonna's house miraculously appeared in Loreto, an ancestor was among the sixteen deputies dispatched to Dalmatia and Palestine to confirm its supernatural departure from those lands. God was less attentive to his descendants' property. The family seat at Recanati was a tumble-down palazzo, its only boast an extensive but neglected library.

Count Monaldo, the poet's father, was a snuff-colored man of threadbare elegance. Dressed head to foot in faded black, he wore patched knee-breeches and a damaged ceremonial sword. During hunting season, he carried a rusty gun and was shadowed by a toothless hound. If shooting had been good, he distributed partridges to the poor, who pitied his squalor. One winter evening, in fact, upon encountering a half-naked beggar, the Count withdrew into a shadowed doorway, removed his trousers, and offered them to the wretch. Out of courtesy, the beggar accepted the gift but as soon as possible disposed it in the trash. Blissfully ignorant, the Count wrapped his legs in a cloak and returned home with starchy dignity, to be upbraided by his wife.

Contessa Adelaide kept Monaldo on a short leash. A strict housekeeper, she was determined to restore her family's fortune *scudo* by *scudo*. If Monaldo needed pocket money, he conspired with the bailiff to sell a barrel of wine behind her back or borrowed cash by pretending to buy books from his own library. The Contessa was not a woman so much as the figurehead of a man-o'-war. Her wooden face was made to frighten pirates, and her prow-shaped bosom carved a wake in the most crowded room. Cold and gray, her eyes shriveled the soul at a glance.

"And yet," Leopardi recalled, "she tried to love me. You must understand, Marchesa, she was deeply religious, an utter excess of Christian perfection. You cannot imagine the severity with which she regulated every detail of our lives. She felt duty-bound to show us the way to heaven, even if it meant dragging us through hell. She imposed a regimen of fasts and prayers. She made us confess our faults at breakfast and spurred us to self-improvement. She always emphasized life's transience. True happiness, she believed, is impossible on earth. If she learned of a child's death, she gave thanks. Spared sin and suffering, it had returned unspotted to God. Beauty she considered a misfortune and rejoiced when my spine curved. She even encouraged me to slouch so I could exaggerate my condition. Mortify the flesh! She measured the poulterer's eggs with a small wooden hoop to guard me against gluttony. I don't know how I outgrew my overcoat, but she forbade a new one, instructing the tailor to lengthen the old one with a strip of sackcloth. God, she reminded me, does not judge by appearances. Even so, I wore a priest's habit until my confirmation."

"That must have helped the budget," I gibed.

"What?" asked the poet, his expression as perplexed as that of his long-lost self.

"Nothing," I said. Why disillusion him more? Fanatics are easier to forgive than misers.

Incidentally, after Leopardi's death, Contessa Adelaide finally succeeded in restoring the family fortune. Still indomitable, she renovated the palazzo and received many dignitaries. She thrilled when the papal nuncio kissed her hand. But her son's growing fame neither softened her flinty piety, nor dispelled her fear and shame that he had squandered his gifts and flouted God. When a literary admirer, whom I had met in Naples, made a pilgrimage to Recanati, the Contessa showed him her son's bedroom, perfectly preserved. Overcome with emotion, the admirer pointed to Leopardi's boyhood portrait and gushed: "Blessed be she who bore thee!"

This annunciation chilled his hostess. Austere and statuesque, crowned with frosty hair, the Contessa neither bent nor turned her head. Instead, she raised her eyes to heaven and said: "God forgive him!"

Door leading into Villa Palagonia's
Hall of Mirrors.

Chapter III
"Heroes and Tenors"

GOD FORGIVE US ALL. HOW ELSE can we forgive Him, for sending us into this world? Life has its pleasures, granted; but even the most passionate life ends like a burp after a feast — a tangy but fleeting residue. Just as dreams haunt a suckling child, a vague jumble, such are the memories left to the dead of their former lives.

But our plight is yours. Among the living, memories and desires confuse perception. Wishes are mistaken for causes. An epileptic falls off a horse and claims lightning has struck. A love-starved girl finds moisture on a statue and pretends the Madonna has wept. The truth brings grief and despair. Such is our disappointment when we learn that the connections between our experiences, the links between our thoughts, exist solely within ourselves and are subject to the fickle disposition of the mind. What fools! We create gods out of our blindness and then curse them for being blind!

"Mankind," Sir William Hamilton told my father, "never tires of idols."

He revered Lord Bacon and preached against four delusions. The *idols of the tribe*, deceptions inherent in the human mind, belong to the entire race. Tricks of sight, for example. The *idols of the cave* arise within a peculiar individual, such as a desperate miner mistaking fool's gold for a fortune. The *idols of the marketplace* result from the false significance bestowed upon words, the seductions of debate and semantics. All Sicily, he said, was addicted to this vice. Finally, the *idols of the theater* come from the sophistry and chicanery infecting theology, philosophy, and science. Defended by the learned, these lies are accepted by the masses. False superstructures are raised on false foundations, and empty systems parade their grandeur on the world's stage.

"Therefore, child," he concluded, looking down his beaky nose and patting my head, "weigh and measure everything. Trust only what can be seen, and take nobody's word."

Fine advice, coming from cuckold.

∾ "Perhaps," Papà confided, after the Cavaliere had excused himself to greet the king, "his *ménage à trois* is a controlled experiment. He often discusses motion and inertia."

I bit my lip to keep from giggling. The masque was about to begin, scenes from Sicilian mythology set to excerpts from Gluck and Rameau. Ferdinand and Maria Carolina had fled Caserta to escape the Pathenopean Republic and had established a temporary court in Palermo. The King and Queen would be back in Naples before the Feast of San Gennaro, Admiral Nelson assured;

but until then, they required constant distraction to ward off despair. Fortunately, it was Carnival and Papà, with the help of Cavaliere Hamilton, had arranged this entertainment to show off his inventions. Stepping forward, dressed in a fillet and a Greek tunic, I bowed to Their Majesties and introduced the mimes and dances.

As the chamber orchestra began the overture to *Iphigenia in Tauris*, a basket filled with wheat rose from the stage. Demeter emerged, joined by Persephone. Then the Graces entered with a mechanical reaper and harvested the wheat, after which Persephone picked poppies before being abducted by Hades in a chariot. Jove thundered disapproval, but when lightning struck, it was conducted to the ground by a metal rod. Next, Daedalus and Icarus fled Crete for Sicily, not on wax pinions but in small boats unfurling wing-like sails. When Icarus disembarked, he fell from the dock into the Bay of Palermo. Quickly, Daedalus donned a diving suit and tried rescuing his son but, alas, was too late. Buoyed by inflatable bladders, the boy's body drifted out to sea as a chorus of mermaids sang a dirge.

Then the scenery switched to Vulcan's smithy under Mt. Etna, and the Cyclops performed a shambling dance. At last, the finale! As a glass harmonica warbled, Papà released the animated carts. Tiny and golden, with delicate spokes, they moved by themselves and rolled down the stage. Each cart brimmed with trays of food, octopus salad, *caponata*, honeyed almonds, and was sniffed by the King's big nose. The court applauded. "A marvel!" Lady

Hamilton exclaimed, at which I turned to the Cavaliere. We had rehearsed all afternoon. He smiled and nodded, and I recit in English:

> *"This day no common task our labour claims;*
> *Full twenty tripods for this hall we've framed,*
> *That placed on living wheels of massy gold,*
> *(Wondrous to tell!) instinct with spirit rolls*
> *From place to place around the blessed abodes,*
> *Self-moved, obedient to the beck of gods. ..."*

The performance ended with a *tableau*: Venus and Mars caught in Vulcan's net with Mercury looking on. "An allegory," I explained. "Love and War defeated by Science, to the delight of Commerce." The Queen and Milady laughed while the Cavaliere resembled a piece of *verde antique*. Admiral Nelson, stolid as ever, massaged his stump.

∽A fine show, but Sir William hated the expense. He dismissed the affair as *spagnolismo*, so much Latin pageantry. Why dress words in spectacle? Let the bare facts speak for themselves. But Papà defended the custom. Pride alone cannot explain it, for pomp reminds us of death. How does your Shakespeare put it? *Our revels now are ended*. We are shadows and will melt into air, into thin air, and like the baseless fabric of this vision, the cloud-capped towers, the gorgeous palaces, the solemn temples, the great globe itself, *si*, and all that it inherit, shall dissolve and, like this insubstantial pageant faded, leave not a rack behind.

"We are such stuff as dreams are made on, and our little life is rounded with a sleep."

At the opera, I would dream wide-awake. After Papà died, I bought a private box in the Teatro Carolino. Wit made me heartless in public, and disappointment with my hare-brained son had killed all private tenderness. That curtained box, therefore, protected by the seal of Trinàcria, became a sanctuary for my emotions. Cocooned in darkness, I could surrender myself to music.

My favorite composer was Vincenzo Bellini, whose work I praised in a series of anonymous articles, but I never admitted this. Because I prided myself on a bone-dry mind, the result of a rigorous scientific education, I was mortified to be drawn to Bellini's melting moods. Such delicacy! If I poked that gossamer web of sound, my finger touched dew. Notes dripped in my heart like juice from a ripe melon, dappled my brain like sunlit beads of moisture on old wallpaper. To keep from swooning, I contrasted the music with its creator.

When we first met in Naples, Bellini was the scholarship boy at the Conservatory of San Sebastiano. Tall and reedy, he was a bit of a mollycoddle. His blue eyes were limpid but vague, and discontent suffused his pale face like cinnamon stirred in hot milk. Rubbing his cleft chin, his one masculine feature, he forever moaned about money. His stipend from the Catania town council covered only his tuition and board, so I provided him with pocket money, fitted him with a wardrobe, and showed him off at the most influential coffee houses.

"We Sicilians must stick together," I said.

My protégé proved a poseur, however. He wore melancholy like a cologne. His hair was dressed in such a romantically wistful fashion, his suit fitted his fragile frame so caressingly and he carried his little Malacca cane in such an idyllic manner that he reminded everyone of the young shepherds in the pastorales at Caserta. "Can't you see him," I asked, "mincing about with a beribboned crook, wearing a pastel jacket and breeches?" His gait was so maidenly, so elegiac and ethereal that he was little more than a sigh in pumps and silk stockings. But his wistful music haunted and comforted my old age.

During a rare truce, Regina and I spent a tranquil afternoon in the conservatory. Ciccio had gone to Monreale on business, and Tiluzzo pressed a cold compress against my brow. As a breeze billowed the curtains, Regina sat at the piano and played *La Sonnambula*. Amina the sleepwalker, betrayed in love, contemplates a faded bouquet: *"Ah, non credea mirarti, sì presto estinto, o fior."* I scarcely could believe you would die so soon, o flower. They chiseled that on Bellini's grave. "Your immense gift condemns you to die young," I had teased in Naples. "Like Raphael, Mozart, or Jesus." He blushed, but the joke proved prophetic. He died at thirty-three, and not of something gentle and lingering but of dysentery. The sheets were soaked in filth.

A solitary tear trickled down my cheek, and Tiluzzo wiped it. Regina noticed, stopped playing, and closed the fallboard.

"That's enough now," she said. "Too morbid."

She preferred a good march ...

∽ "Left right, left right! On to glory, my son!"

They had spent hours learning those drills: shoulder, load, present arms. Tiluzzo looked so bewildered with that broom, so cranky and confused from missing his nap that I grunted for them to stop. But who could hear anything over that pounding? Regina was fit to wake the dead.

> *Si scopron le tombe, si levano i morti!*
> *I martiri nostri son tutti risorti! ...*

When Tiluzzo bawled, she scooped him into her lap and sat in the rocker for another lesson. Ignore history, she told him. History will claim that Garibaldi never set foot in Villabate, that his troops came down the Mezzagno side of Mount Griffone. Written by Northerners, such history wished to diminish Sicily's contribution to that glorious campaign. Ask anyone in town. They all saw him! That's why she had put that plaque in the square of the General's words to Lieutenant Bixio: *"Nino, oggi qui, domani a Palermo."* Today here, tomorrow Palermo.

She went to the wall map, wielded a pointer, and traced the path of the General's march. After landing at Marsala, the Red Shirts advanced to Rapingallo and Salemi, conquered Calatafimi, stormed through Alcamo, Partinico, and Parco before the carnage at Piana dei Greci, reconnoitered Marineo, then scouted the hills between Misilmeri and Gibilrossa to prepare for the Siege of Palermo. All Villabate had known the Thousand were near, and Coffaro the innkeeper had smuggled them fresh supplies and ammunition. On the morning of May 26, 1860 (*She's a big one for dates,* I thought), a messenger arrived announcing that Garibaldi would stop in town to express his personal thanks. The town was thrown into a frenzy of preparation.

"Great Grandma barricaded herself in the villa and forbade me to go." (*And I was right! Cheer the gaucho who had come to destroy our way of life?*) "Threatened to strip me naked before the servants and whip me with her rosary. But jubilation had made me fearless. I snatched a bunch of roses from the table and ran to the piazza. The Red Shirts were already there, with their wild beards and Enfield rifles, and the General was clapping Coffaro's shoulder and shaking his hand. He was saying something, I don't know what. I only knew I had to see him, but I was so nervous I mispronounced his name: '*Viva Galibardo!*' And I butted through the crowd, threw myself in his arms, and exploded like a grenade of roses. '*Viva Galibardo!*' I cried. Everybody laughed, and the General roared like a tickled bull."

"Galibardo," he said. "So that's my name, eh?" Then he realized she was scarred and stunted, and his eyes filled with compassion. They were brown, incidentally, not blue like in the posters. But no one had looked at her that way before, and she fell in love on the spot. I could understand why. Even at a distance, he was a handsome man. His face was so ruddy. His long hair blazed, and his teeth were pearls amid the coral of his beard.

"And what is your name, child?" I heard him ask.

"Regina!" she crowed.

"Regina," he said, "a little queen. *Are* you a little queen?"

"Her grandmother's a Bourbon, General," Coffaro said. "Thinks you should be hung."

My carriage was at the other end of the piazza, and I glared out the window. *"Passa Savoia!"* I shouted, shaking my fist. Savoy passes. An old Sicilian curse. When that popinjay, Victor Amadeus of Savoy, assumed the crown of Sicily, he came to our island in pomp and crossed it from end to end. His passage was followed by the worst famine in living memory. Seven months later, the king returned to Turin, but the saying *"Passa Savoia!"* remained behind, a malediction against disasters and foreigners. "Go back to your goats on Caprera!" I railed. "You are an Attila, and your men are Huns!"

Grumbling in the ranks. Regina's expression faltered, but she stood her ground. One soldier, a pimply Sicilian, spewed oaths in her face. Worse might have followed, if the General had not raised his hand for silence.

"A child of privilege who fights for freedom is welcome in this army," he said. He leaned over, his expression kind, and asked: "Whose flag do you fight under?"

"Yours, General! Yours!" And she tore a strip from her red petticoat and waved it like a banner, hopping and shouting: '*Viva* Galibardo! *Viva* the Thousand!'

The Red Shirts laughed and whooped.

"A recruit. Do you know how to be a soldier, my dear?"

"I nodded, borrowed a rattan cane from an old man, and pretended it was a rifle. I shouldered arms, drilled. 'Bang, bang, bang! Bang, bang, bang!' I wiped the cane with my bit of petticoat and presented arms to the General.

"'Tennnnnnnnnn-*tion!*' I snapped to and stood silent. The General glanced at a kepi-clad officer with a big nose and a waxed moustache. This was Bixio. 'Nino,' he said, and indicated something with a toss of the head. Bixio went to the General's saddle and fetched a folded piece of cloth. With a snap of the wrists, Garibaldi unfurled it. It was a red tunic.

"'Private Regina: step forward!'

"I obeyed, trembling. The General dressed me in the tunic and roughly kissed my cheeks. 'Tiny warrior,' he whispered in my ear. His beard tickled my neck, and I whimpered and buried my face in his chest. Enfolding me tenderly, he turned to his troops. 'Men,' he said, 'greet your new comrade in arms!' Laughing, he lifted me squealing over his head as the Red Shirts fired their rifles in the air. ... Then we feasted. The entire village."

Flies droned in the parlor, and Tiluzzo nibbled honey puffs and drowsed. But Regina was oblivious to the heat. Her arms crisscrossed her tunic, a gesture of self-consecration.

"That day," she murmured, "I was covered in glory."

"That day," Ciccio said, "you were covered in welts."

He had entered the parlor, eating a pomegranate and spitting pits. We exchanged looks, a rare moment of collusion. Our expressions asked the same question: *Is she deliberately lying?*

We had witnessed the whole scene. There were no cheers, no rifle shots, no glory. She confected these fantasies while I whipped her with my rosary. She taunted me with them, which made me whip her harder. (How the blood stained the ivory!) Yes, Garibaldi had accepted and thanked her for the flowers, but he had not given Regina the tunic. He was too preoccupied mapping the route to Palermo. It had been the Sicilian private, the one who had cursed her, who made amends by giving her his shirt. But why should she remember him? Garibaldi looked like a god, the private like a prickly pear. Ciccio smirked and whispered in my ear, but loud enough for her to hear: "If *I* had whipped her, she wouldn't talk such nonsense."

Stone-faced, Regina mounted the rocker, but Ciccio lifted Tiluzzo from her lap and set him on the piano. He was almost gentle.

"Listen, Priest Face. Any idiot can look special on a horse. I make carriages, so I should know. I, too, saw Garibaldi. I, too, was impressed. Until your Grandpa Nino wised me up. We were digging ditches along the road to Palermo — we hadn't been invited to that little *festa*, Regina — when the Red Shirts marched by. Northerners, all right. You could tell from their talk. They had straws up their noses. Mostly lawyers and shopkeepers, too, from the way they looked at us. Garibaldi raised his hand, and the battalion stopped. He trotted over and saluted your Grandpa. He was a fine-looking man, Regina, before he died of overwork.

"'You!' said the General. 'You have the body of a hero! Out of that ditch and leave the dirt! Come with us to glory!' Papa said nothing. He just looked at Garibaldi and flicked his chin. Safeties clicked, and I thought for sure they would massacre us. But my father just stood there … like a post. Then one said: 'He's a *terrone*, boys, a dirt eater. Save your bullets.' Garibaldi huffed and spurred his horse, and off they marched, singing Verdi.

"Meanwhile, Papa had returned to work. I was young and stupid, so I asked why he had done that. And Papa said: 'Because when Italy will be free, I'll still be digging this ditch.'"

Regina had turned away. She rocked in the chair as if escaping with you on horseback.

"The butcher wants to be paid," Ciccio said. "If that's alright by you."

Regina said nothing and rocked. Ciccio chuckled bitterly, shook his head, and shut the door. When he was gone, Regina reined in her imaginary horse and said: "Don't listen to him, Tiluzzo. Great men glorify us all."

∽Do they? I doubt it. But she was an incorrigible hero-worshiper. She spent the rest of her life awaiting Garibaldi's return. How can any woman place her faith in a mere man? It baffles me. My father's generation was indifferent to heroes, but mine craved them like sweets. Even poor Bellini was not immune to the bugle's call.

During his homecoming tour, I held a reception for the Swan of Sicily at Villabate. The chef served a tub of spaghetti Norma, the new pasta dish named after his latest triumph. We had been forced to use eggplants from the greenhouse because the ones in the field would not ripen until Pentecost, thanks to an unusually cool spring. Happily, the guests were too tipsy to notice. Don Benjamin had supplied the wine. Unable to bear a grudge, unless money was involved, he had forgiven me years ago and beamed his approval, but the sight of Donna Alessandra on his arm pained me. Perhaps too flippantly, I declared: "Ambrosia! Apollo and his muses thank you!"

A claque of rowdy young noblemen surrounded Bellini. Normally pink, his cheeks were as livid as peaches soaked in sangria.

"Apollo and his muses," Don Benjamin said, "will have a headache tomorrow."

The town band played a thumping march. Bellini must have liked this vulgar tune because two years later he adapted it for *I Puritani*, a work I utterly detest. What could be more absurd than an opera set during the English Civil Wars? *L'Anglia terra ha libertà! A Cromvello eterna gloria!* Well, anything sounds convincing sung in Italian.

Pounding the table, my younger guests were delighted with themselves. Some were former Carbonari, who welcomed this chance to vent their patriotism. Sound the trumpet! Fight intrepidly! How beautiful to face death shouting freedom! I indulged these high spirits, until one Adonis proclaimed Sicilian independence. "Drunk with freedom, gentlemen? Even after the English constitution ruined our estates?"

The band stopped playing. My outburst had disturbed the guests, although not nearly as much as my face. Due to eyestrain, I wore smoked glasses, which gave me the appearance of a *jettatore*, someone with the evil eye. Bellini made horns at me, but the young Adonis stood firm. His hair was black and slick, his chin slightly truculent, but he was gallant and good-natured for all that.

"You admire the English," he tactfully reminded me.

Don Benjamin accepted this compliment with a nod. This display of good manners softened my severity. "Admiration is fine," I said. "Even emulation. But you, signor, advocate immolation."

"And why not?" he said. "Isn't liberty worth any price?"

"Provided we pay our own way. But when we ask others to pay for us ..." I left the sentence unfinished and offered more wine.

"Nothing wrong with self-interest, lad," Don Benjamin said. "In business or in life. Keeps us human. Only fanatics think otherwise, and fanatics hate liberty."

"I see your point," the young man conceded. "I'm an individualist, too. But shouldn't men unite for a noble cause? Shouldn't they be willing to sacrifice themselves?"

"No!" I bristled. "What an absurd expectation!"

His knitted brows formed a hole between his eyes. He would be shot during the uprising. "Then you don't believe in heroes," he said, nearly pouting.

"Only at the opera. There they sing on key, and the management provides a libretto."

∽Rehearsals for *Un Ballo in Maschera* had ground to a halt. Incensed because the six thousand ducats for the piano rehearsals remained in arrears, Maestro Verdi threatened to quit: "You steal my time, and you steal my money! I won't work with thieves!"

A major donor, I was entitled to a stage pass at the San Carlo. After the Carolino closed, I had been compelled to ferry to Naples, if I wanted to go to the opera. It was rarely to my taste. Good singing had been replaced by nationalistic grandstanding. Verdi was a bandmaster, his music fit only for train stations, but his backstage tantrums always entertained me.

Verdi demanded to examine his contract, and a brow-beaten prompter brought him a rickety table. Seated in the middle of the stage, a vindictive attorney rather than an exacting composer, he hunted for a loophole. The intensity tortured the easy-going Neapolitans. Verdi cracked his knuckles, rattled papers, sharpened pencils, ground his teeth, and constricted his shaggy eyebrows as he gleaned the fine print. I nudged my granddaughter.

"The dragon in his lair," I whispered. "Confront him, *cara*. You're armed, after all."

She held a bouquet of gold-tipped gladioli and wore a fisher-girl costume for Carnival. With complete confidence, she approached the Maestro and held out the flowers. At first, Verdi was too absorbed in the contract, but the fragrance soon caught his attention. He raised his eyes, blinked, and stroked his beard.

"An admirer, Pasticcio," Signora Verdi said.

As the Bear of Busseto rose, the girl curtsied and presented the flowers. Surprised but charmed, Verdi bowed and accepted her tribute. The jowly stage manager complimented me.

"A remarkable child. How old?" he asked.

"Ten on the first of May."

"She seems older. Her name?"

"Regina," I said.

He nodded approvingly. "She's a little queen, alright."

Her father Alvarito had named her Regina Carolina, after his royal godmother, but we called her Quarantotta, Miss Forty-Eight. Born in that year of revolution, when Ruggiero Settimo declared Sicilian independence and Bourbon cannons bombarded Messina and Palermo, Regina was a firecracker with flaming red hair and an explosive temper. She would have been beautiful, if not for the mark on her right cheek, which resembled a dueling scar. At her First Communion party, Concetta, her rabbit-faced mother, had told her to behave. The little savage practically had to be straitjacketed into her dress; now she was sulking over dessert. Concetta pinched her cheek. "You'll never marry," she teased, "unless you learn to smile."

The child glared, rose from her seat, and walked to the buffet. With an expression of stony contempt, she picked up a knife and cut herself, exactly where Concetta had pinched her. The guests gasped.

"I won't smile," Regina said. "And I won't marry."

She returned to her seat and finished her cake, blood staining her white communion dress. Concetta was distraught. "No man will ever look at her!" she wailed.

"Lucky girl," I said, and kissed Regina's bleeding cheek.

I wanted her all to myself, as compensation for years of disappointment. Our family's status had declined. With the abolishment of primogeniture, large estates had been parceled out to a pack of barking cousins. The entire clan —Valanguerras and Brancifortes, Spinellis and Belmontes— settled into shabby gentility. They were content to chew fava beans, provided their tapestries were not too faded and their carriages not too squeaky. My property alone had value, and it was doomed to go to Alvarito, a complete idiot! I could not disinherit him because he was such a devoted son. The scandal would have disgraced my memory. Instead, I pretended to teach him how to manage our affairs and nursed a grudge.

His presence offended me. His watery eyes were set too close together. His chin was flabbier than melted wax, his hair as patchy as dying parsley. Timid as a boy, he grew conceited after marriage, thanks to Concetta's dowry. Every week he took the steamer to Naples to prove he and that poor ninny were society. They were too frumpy for Caserta, from whence I was still banished because of what had occurred at the late king's wake, so they haunted the San Carlo. The ushers warily accepted their tips but avoided touching them because they were jinxed. Broken props, snapped fiddle strings, and laryngitis followed in their wake. Composers dreaded their backstage visits.

During the Act One intermission at the premiere of *Luisa Miller*, they ambushed Verdi. They fussed and flattered. Such lovely music! With the Maestro's kind permission, could they play that opening aubade at the silver anniversary mass for Concetta's parents? Her mother's name was also Luisa! Wasn't that a charming coincidence? Verdi tugged and began extracting himself when some scenery snapped from the ceiling and crashed inches behind him. Enraged, he ordered the Belmontes evicted from the theatre. Parasites! Ghouls! Get out!

Despite the rough treatment, and a parting salvo of Parmesan curses, they acted as if they were being honored. The next morning, they were dead, having contracted cholera from tainted sherbet purchased at the lobby refreshment stand. The health inspector disposed of the bodies, so we never held a funeral. Nevertheless, for a whole year I visited the chapel daily and lit a candle, grateful because Regina had been delivered from her parents.

Lively and precocious, my granddaughter spent hours burrowing in the library, which included a first edition of Pope's Homer from Lord Hamilton and an autographed copy of Leopardi's *Moral Essays*. But Regina preferred

Alfieri and Mazzini. At eight, she proclaimed herself a Republican and vowed to name her son after Atilius Regulus, the Roman commander who returned to Carthage to face certain torture and death rather than break his oath. I never took these declarations seriously. They seemed romantic, not political, inspired by animal passion rather than genuine conviction. Significantly, her patriotism intensified after her first period, which came unusually early. Restless and frustrated, she stomped through our villa, squinting and clenching her fists. Footsteps constantly echoed on the tiles, or another porcelain figurine shattered because once again she had bumped into an end table. Finally, I had enough.

"By the end of the year," I announced, "either buy a pair of glasses or take a lover! If you take a lover, skip the glasses. Men are best seen as a blur."

My ultimatum failed to amuse her. She had no sense of humor, only a hothouse pride. Her stiff spine, her flashing eyes seemed to say: *I will give myself to no man, unless he is a hero.* Italy was her true love. When I discovered miniatures of Verdi and Garibaldi in her bedroom shrine, I shook my head. You're heading for grief, Quarantotta. How could I disillusion her? After learning that Verdi was returning to the San Carlo, I booked our passage on the steamer. Let the silly goose learn first-hand what shits heroes can be.

∽The plan did not succeed as I had anticipated. Enchanting in her fisher-girl costume, Regina had captivated

Signora Verdi. At least, that was what people called her. For me, she was still Giuseppina Strepponi, the former diva, who had ruined her voice and had disowned her bastards for Verdi's sake. After a decade together, she and the Maestro were still unmarried, and everyone knew the union would remain childless. So when she shyly requested that Regina attend future rehearsals, Verdi consented, as either a token of affection or a concession for his peace of mind.

Regina mitigated the tedium of rehearsals. I expected her to moon and mope, but instead she behaved perfectly, as much to vex me as to please her idol. Usually grave and mature, she was content to be a child. She swapped nursery rhymes with La Strepponi, marked time with the concertmaster, and minded Loulou, Verdi's white Maltese. He and Regina shared the same bangs, snappy black eyes, and pert nose. She curled and ribboned Loulou's hair and, during breaks, played hide and seek with him behind the scenery. If Verdi encouraged her high spirits, she skipped and sang; but whenever the Maestro became bearish, she sat still and kept quiet. At such times, she gravitated towards the cartoonist Melchiorre Delfico.

Short and trim, with a perfumed Vandyke, Delfico had been assigned to cover the rehearsals by *La Gazzetta Napoletana*. Delfico filled his sketchbook with caricatures: Verdi in a stovepipe hat and Strepponi, voluminous in black crinoline, disembarking at the Bay of Naples; Verdi, in the Blue Grotto, brandishing a torch and riding piggyback on a guide; Verdi in his nightcap instructing sleepy Neapolitans how to cook risotto. During the Sicilian revolt, I had contributed mordant political cartoons to *Il Don Pirlone* — a horned Ruggiero Settimo butting Punchinello off the cliffs of Messina, a three-legged lamb devoured by wolves wearing the Order of San Gennaro — but nothing this clever or elegant.

"*Cedo junioribus*," I said. I yield to the younger generation.

Whenever Delfico finished a drawing, he showed it to Regina, who giggled, clapped, and brought the drawing to Verdi. More often than not, this relay saved somebody's hide. Hounded by the censors, who objected to an aristocrat being assassinated on stage, and nettled by salary disputes, Verdi looked for any excuse to storm like King Lear. One particularly awful afternoon, he flayed the chorus alive. Imbeciles! Cretins! Fools! Did they know why they croaked like a frog pond? Because they were all Spanish toadies!

Thunderstruck silence. Regina flounced over and rustled a sheet of paper.

"What is it, child?"

She handed him a drawing. It showed Verdi, his mane disarrayed, stamping and flinging his arms like a wild man. Lear chuckled, despite himself.

"And do I really look like this?" he asked.

"Oh no, Maestro. Much meaner."

Delfico and Strepponi roared. The chorus joined in, and the theater rang with laughter. As the accompanist played the downbeat, the tenors and basses sang: *Ve', la tragedia mutò in commedia.* How quickly tragedy turns to farce ...

> *Ha, ha, ha!*
> *Ha, ha, ha!*
> *Ha, ha, ha, ha!*
> *E che baccano sul caso strano*
> *E che commenti per la città!*

After rehearsal, Verdi was accosted by two rich admirers — a florid banker and his mincing wife — at the back door. Forced to leave in their company, Verdi endured their drivel, and pretended not to notice Strepponi's longing glances at Regina. Outside the San Carlo, a group of street urchins waved sparklers and whistled to get our attention. On the wall, they scribbled "VIVA V.E.R.D.I.!" It was an acronym for *"Viva Vittorio Emanuele, Re d'Italia!"* Long live Victor Emmanuel, King of Italy. Verdi's chest swelled. The revolution was the real opera, he told Regina. What is music to the sound of guns? Regina borrowed Delfico's charcoal pencil and joined the urchins. She scrawled: "VIVA V.E.R.D.I.!"

The banker's wife simpered and said: "Oh, isn't that charming, Tito? Let's do it, too!" She stole chalk from one of the urchins. Her hand fluttered and wrote in showy script: "VIVA VERDI!" The banker did the same. "We honor you, Maestro!" they declared. Verdi hated their tribute. He gnashed his teeth as they laughed like children and covered the wall with their blasted VIVA VERDIs. Grim and silent, the urchins stood apart, their hands shoved in their pockets. Walking their beat, two *carabinieri* stopped and observed the graffitists, cynically amused.

Verdi boiled, and rightly so. If the fools had understood the meaning of those words, they would have slashed their wrists and written the letters in their blood. Still, the irony was too delicious to resist, and I approached the Maestro and offered my congratulations.

"You're their idol," I said.

"God help me then," he mumbled.

Regina turned to us, proud and accomplished; one hand holding the charcoal pencil, the other a burning sparkler. But her triumph was short-lived. The next day Verdi broke his contract and left Naples. The authorities had discredited him. Delfico's caricatures appeared in *La Gazzetta*, and everyone at the café laughed, including the banker and his wife. If I had not restrained her, Regina would have scratched out their eyes. She wept tears of rage, until I slapped her across the mouth. As she staunched her bleeding lip with a napkin, I called for the check.

"Let that be a lesson to you," I said. "No man can be a hero to a cartoonist."

❧ "I want a hero, an uncommon want ...

> *When every year and month sends forth a new one,*
> *Till, after cloying the gazettes with cant,*
> *The age discovers he is not a true one ..."*

"Brava, Marchesa!"

Leopardi clapped feebly, not from boredom but fatigue. I flourished my fan and bowed, biding my time to strike. Meanwhile, it was a pleasure speaking English. The language of precision and rationality, he called it. He welcomed the opportunity to practice.

"Byron was right, of course," he said. "Nowadays heroes are manufactured for the newspapers. The age of Homer is over, Signora."

"And good riddance! An age of barbarism. Voltaire was right. He had a jaded opinion of the Greeks. Beauty, yes. They had plenty of beauty. But no science."

"True," he said, "beauty but no science. And yet the Greeks left their mark on Sicily. Your island is full of glorious ruins."

"Ruins aren't glorious, Contino, only burdensome. Particularly when they're not yours. They make one morbid. The past never dies in Sicily, though God knows it tries."

"Time," he mused, "dissolves all human structures ... except castles in the air."

"You smile," I said sharply. "Ruins amuse you?" I still seethed over that epigram.

Leopardi shook his head. He was weary again. He squeezed my hand, but I barely felt it. From his weakness or my numbness, who could tell? "Life amuses me, Marchesa," he said. "But only children can laugh at it without breaking their hearts."

More self-pity. It marred even his poetry. "I'd rather not talk about children, thank you."

"Because you dislike them?"

"Because I pity them. They're cursed with belief."

"And we with unbelief. Which do you think is the greater sin?"

An odd way of putting it! He puzzled me. According to Ranieri, the Count had been such a devout child that he wouldn't step on floor joints out of reverence for the Cross. I believe it. He still had the dress and manners of a priest — a poor country priest reeking of tripe and onions. Puh! The odor of sanctity. My mother had the same smell, no matter how often she used orange water and lavender salts. We bathed together every day. I remember her soft cool hands and little crucifix. She had mismatched eyes, one green and one blue, and at siesta filled my head with angels:

> Dormi nicuzza ccu l'angili tò,
> Dormi e riposa, ti cantu la vò.
> Vò , vò, vò,
> Dormi bedda e fa' la vò.
> Vò, vò, vò,
> Dormi bedda e fa' la vò.

Mad, of course. She had to be mad to love us the way she did, forgiving Papà's infidelities and my contempt. The convent became her asylum. As her mind deteriorated, she conversed with Catherine of Siena and rode in Elijah's chariot. To cure these fits, the doctors prescribed a diet of cherries and passed magnets over her body. But the nuns encouraged her to write down her visions. Before she died, she sent me her journal and a copy of *Interior Castles*. I burned them both, unread.

"Belief," I replied. "It makes one more vulnerable. Believe nothing and no one, Contino."

Leopardi nodded. "Yes, that's the difference. Children find everything in nothing; adults find nothing in everything."

"You should write that down."

"I already have," he said.

I laughed, despite myself, which eased the tension. *Good*, I thought. *I'll turn this detente to my advantage.* "You know, Contino, I think *you* believe."

"I'm afraid not, Marchesa. I doubt everything—including my own doubt. But I was trained to believe."

"All children," I said, "are trained to believe."

"Not the way I was." He smiled ironically. "My father wanted me to be Defender of the Faith. I lived in his library and studied Chrysostum in Greek. I was to be a great apologist, you see. Papà even got a dispensation so I could read forbidden books. 'Learn the errors of the godless and correct them, Giacomino.' Such was my childhood. I worked ten, eleven hours daily. It wrecked my health and nearly blinded me. In the end, I became a skeptic, I'm afraid. I lost my faith, but I did gain this."

With mock affection, he patted his hump.

"Even the ugliest deformity is superior to the most beautiful illusion."

"You're wrong," he said. "Without beautiful illusions, life becomes purposeless. Without his illusions, Columbus could not have discovered America."

"Which he mistook for India. That only proves my point!"

"You don't think much of great men, do you, Marchesa?"

"I don't think much of men at all. I've had too many lovers."

Yes, I fumed, *Trinàcria delving in her Ovid.*

"And yet yours was an era of great men."

"Hmph!"

"Napoleon ..."

"That Corsican upstart! Spoke execrable French."

"Admiral Nelson ..."

"A one-armed, one-eyed coxcomb, besotted with a fashionable slattern."

"And yet they were heroes."

"Really, Contino. You're worse than those urchins who gape at Orlando at the marionette show. Can't you see the strings? That's all a hero is, a puppet on a string. Worse, a puppet who refuses to see the string."

∞Leopardi changed the subject, so I knew I was right. And a century of mummification has solidified my opinion. Still, I prefer what that American soldier said when he visited the Cappuccini. He was the son of a Sicilian immigrant from Walt Whitman's Brooklyn. This was shortly after the American invasion.

Two frowzy monks were showing him a crypt reserved for Bourbon officers. "These gallant souls," one said, "gave their lives for God and king."

The other monk crossed himself. "The Madonna shield them forever in her mantle! Where in this Godless age, young man, will you find such selflessness, such sacrifice?"

It was a taunt as well as a reproach, but the soldier ignored it and read the brass marker: *"Colonel Enea Di Giuliano."*

"A great hero," said the first Capuchin. "Died in the Revolution of 1848."

The soldier, an unshaven infantryman, glanced at Colonel Di Giuliano, who looked like a smoked herring in his cocked hat and blue tunic.

"If you say so, brother," the soldier said. "Where I'm from, though, a hero is a sandwich."

I laughed so loud their hair stood on end.

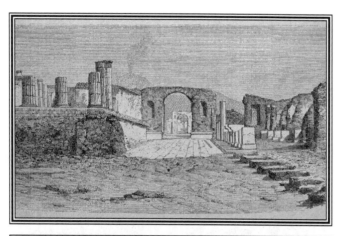

TOP: POMPEII RUINS WITH VESUVIUS IN DISTANCE.
BOTTOM: PLASTER CASTS OF HUMAN REMAINS.

Chapter IV
God the Grocer

 COLD CUTS, THAT'S WHAT WE
are. Time approaches God's counter and
bawls: "I'm starved! Make me a *panino!*"
And God forces us through a slicer and
slaps us between two hunks of bread.
Some sandwiches are all tongue, others all rump, but
Time is not picky and swallows everything. So did we.
Give us this day our daily lie. When we look back on life,
we are astonished and ashamed. And such, to the living,
must death appear.

Our descendants troop through the catacombs and
cross themselves. Like good Sicilians, they carry Mass cards.
Not like the English and American tourists, who carry
insurance cards. My great-grandson shared his with the
mayor. It showed a house nestled in God's palms: "You're
in Good Hands with All State." How can courage survive in a race of underwriters? If Seneca had been obliged
to pay a premium, he never could have been a Stoic.

My generation was reckless and extravagant. Today's
forever counts the cost. Enlightened self-interest, they
call it. Haggling raised to an ethical imperative, more
likely. Grocers, even with their intimates, they weigh
and measure, price and sell. If everyone profits from an

emotional transaction, then the greatest good has been
achieved for the greatest number. Bentham's calculus
rules the world. Balanced the books of fate, that
Englishman: *pain for debit, pleasure for credit* ...

∞ "And so, all other things being equal, pushpin is as
good as poetry." Signor Whitaker sipped his tea and
stroked his lynx-like whiskers. They had grown fuller
and fiercer during my absence but still could not camou-
flage that weak chin.

"Very logical and democratic, don't you think?"

A prompt, not a question. Like most intellectual dan-
dies, Signor Whitaker sought my approval by pretending
to ask for my opinion. For Don Benjamin's sake, I had
resisted the temptation to roll my eyes during his panegyric, but he was becoming insufferable.

"Indeed," I said, "but not universal. Signor Bentham's
ideas might not work in Sicily."

"Perhaps you're right, Marchesa," he said. "England
alone appreciates his philosophy and mourns his loss.
His genius epitomizes our race."

"I agree, a purely English phenomenon. A genius by
way of bourgeois stupidity."

Donna Alessandra covered her mouth with her fan
and shook her bare shoulders. Don Benjamin chuckled,
shook his head, and wagged his finger. "Walked right
into that one, Jos."

He enjoyed taking his nephew down a peg. Although
he praised the young man's abilities ("a perfect desk man,"

Don Benjamin called him), he resented his airs and am-
bition. Panting to become partner, the parlor lynx had
begun sniffing around customers and investors. Already
he was becoming popular. Don Benjamin's talent was for
making money, Signor Whitaker's for spending it. Still,
he had lasted longer than his predecessor, a hapless older
brother, who had died upon reaching Palermo. "Your
son is dead," Don Benjamin wrote his sister. "Send me
another." This callousness perhaps explained Signor
Whitaker's dark moods. He was so dour, with his hooded eyes and bitter mouth, that even his mighty uncle
sometimes feared him. For now, the young malcontent
sulked and slurped his tea.

We sat and ate pistachio ice cream in the drawing
room of Don Benjamin's townhouse, wedged between
Via Bara and Via Lampedusa. He planned to buy an 18th-
century villa in the Piano Sant'Oliva, just outside the city
walls, for his wife. Alessandra Spadafora was lucky.
Duchess of Santa Rosalia, she also held a string of other
titles — Baroness of Mazara, Marchesa of Roccella,
Marchesa of San Martino, Princess of Maletto, Princess
of Venetico — but her proudest possession was her wealthy
husband, who had become more Sicilian than she.

Bronzed and haughty, Don Benjamin almost exclu-
sively communicated in the local dialect, reserving English
for business correspondents and pesky relatives. His new-
found dignity pleased me. Awarded the Order of Saint
Ferdinand for his achievements, he wore a blue and red
ribbon in his buttonhole. Strategic donations had made

him Baron of Santa Rosalia, and his coat of arms hung over the carved mantel: golden conch shells against a red field with the motto *"Spes et Fides,"* Hope and Faith. Even so, he missed his native land — that other island, so different from ours — and pumped me for news.

"Was England everything you expected?" he asked.

Actually, no; for my expectations had been based on my father's lectures at the Royal Society and Lady Hamilton's card games with the Prince Regent. London was no longer bright and brittle but dusty and bustling. Under a canopy of steam and soot, the streets flowed with pedestrians and omnibuses. The crush and stench rivaled the stockyards at Kensington. Crowds menaced me in public, boors in private. At the Drury Lane revival of *La Sonnambula*, which Bellini had invited me to review for *Il Giornale Regno delle Due Sicilie*, a hawking laugh drowned out Malibran's singing. In the next box, a beefy Staffordshire manufacturer snorted and spat into a monogrammed handkerchief. When his wife shushed him, he waved her away and rocked in his plush chair. "I can't help it!" he gasped. "It's too absurd!"

He was right. The performance was in English and had drained the music of its poetry. The tenderest sentiments became ridiculous. I felt ridiculous, too. Bejeweled ladies whispered and pointed at me. Dressed in a feathered turban and a paisley shawl, I could not have been more conspicuous if I had worn a sandwich board and sold Italian ices. "My dear," one solicitous matron said during the intermission, "this isn't Brighton in the old days."

The new king was nothing like his late brother George, whose gilded grossness rivaled that of the Bourbons. The first Neapolitan to sit on the British throne. King William, however, shunned pomp and mingled with the people. He stood in his carriage and bowed to the crowds as the horses clopped on the cobblestone and spat on the pavement. Silly Billy, they called him. Well, familiarity breeds contempt. Look at the new French king. After the July Revolution, Paris clamored for a bourgeois monarch, so Louis-Philippe, the Citizen King, dressed like a banker. Everyone cheered Philippe Égalité, until he became a target for journalists and cartoonists. Who could resist mocking that pear-shaped face? Without ceremony and distance, the illusion of majesty vanishes.

I nearly disappeared myself. In the street, passers-by looked through me until I was convinced I had become invisible. At salons, monologists acted as if I did not exist. Only twice was I asked a direct question: the first time when a poet solicited an opinion about his ode to Italian unification; the second time when a young heiress sought information about a murder. Apparently, body snatchers in Bethnal Green had knifed a Sicilian waif. Did I by chance know the poor boy? Sicily, I pointed out, was as large as Wales. She blinked and pressed my hand.

"Then surely," she said, "your paths must have crossed."

Depressed, I withdrew to Regent Street, the guest of Charles Cavendish Fulke Greville, Sir William Hamilton's grandnephew, who kept a diary and raced horses. As

Secretary to the Privy Council, Lord Greville informed me of current events, which I shared with Don Benjamin. England, I reported, was expanding its railroads and re-forming Parliament. Sometimes it killed two birds with one stone.

A Signor William Huskisson, former Leader of the Commons and M.P. for Liverpool, had attended the opening of the Liverpool and Manchester Railway. A financier and a two-time Secretary of the Treasury, Huskisson had invested his own capital in the railroad and had urged the public to do likewise. The grateful company award-ed him a seat on its board of directors and invited him to accompany the Duke of Wellington on its flagship engine, the *Northumbrian*.

At Parkside, near Newton-le-Willows in Lancashire, the train stopped to observe a cavalcade on the adjacent line. Several members of Wellington's party stepped onto the line for a closer look. Eager to join them, Huskisson was exiting his car, when another train approached on the parallel track and crushed his leg. A train took the wounded man to Eccles, where he died a few hours later. A tragedy, of course, but the papers cited the remarkable fact that the *Northumbrian*, driven by its inventor George Stephenson, conveyed the unfortunate gentleman a dis-tance of about fifteen miles in twenty-five minutes, or at the rate of thirty-six miles an hour.

The company's stock soared.

∞ "That man died a martyr to progress," Signor Whitaker declared.

"What progress?" I said. "It was an accident."

"There are no accidents, Marchesa. Only the march of history."

"Tell that to Signor Huskisson."

"He would have agreed. We're on the verge of a new millennium."

"Isn't that a bit much, Jos?" Don Benjamin chided.

"Not at all, sir! Sometimes I think you lack vision."

Don Benjamin smiled, unperturbed. His wealth spoke for itself.

"I've never claimed to be an innovator," he said. "I've stood on the shoulders of others. But I had to clamber up their backs to get there."

Donna Alessandra beamed. Her husband was the perfect blend of pride and humility. Because he had copied and improved existing methods, Don Benjamin always credited his rivals for contributing to his success. But he also recognized and understood his own superiority. No one better understood the secret of making money. "Do an ordinary thing extraordinarily well," he once explained, "and people will pay for it."

"Heart of oak," Donna Alessandra said, patting his hand.

"Because I have a clear conscience. As Doctor Johnson observed, there are few ways in which a man can be more innocently employed than in making money."

Yes, but where did he get the capital to start his enterprise? I smiled but said nothing. Rumor claimed that he had never paid back the creditors of his father's and uncle's bank in Leeds, which failed shortly after he had

bought his *baglio*. When a group of London associates
sued, Don Benjamin was already basking in the Sicilian
sun. "I won't go back to Yorkshire," he vowed, "until I
can buy the whole county!" But he never went back, not
even when he had enough money to buy half of England.
If he had, he might have been convicted and sent to the
Marshalsea. Instead, Don Benjamin went native and became a Sicilian aristocrat. Before he died, he built himself
a two-story palazzo off Via Roma, with fourteen balcon-
ies and two grated entrances, north and south, on a busy
square landscaped with palms, yuccas, monkey puzzles,
and tropical plants. Palermo renamed it Piazza Ingham.

"And Dr. Johnson shared my opinion," Signor Whitaker
pursued. "He believed trade would free mankind from
ignorance and poverty."

"Oh come now," I said.

"Think of what it's done here. For the first time, people
have a chance at the good life."

I shook my head. "The good life is more than material decency."

"But it must be based on material decency. Give people
the goods they deserve, and they will decide for themselves how to lead a good life. Don't you agree, uncle?"

"That sounds like religion, Jos, not business," Don
Benjamin said.

"Exactly!" I said. "This is a creed, not a science! You
claim people will decide for themselves how to be good.
According to what values?"

"The values they choose. '*Take what you want and pay
for it.*' Isn't that the proverb?"

"We Sicilians have another proverb: *'Put a price on everything and know the truth.'*"

"What truth?" asked Signor Whitaker. "Whatever validates your class? There is no truth, Marchesa, only self-interest. In the future, we will stop squabbling over truth and learn to deal with utility. People no longer will be asked what they believe in but what they will pay for."

"Signor Bentham again. Then money will become the measure of all things?"

"Why not? It's objective, self-evident, and irrefutable. It will end human conflict."

"But doesn't greed cause war?"

"Only in the past, thanks to scarcity. We have entered an age of abundance. The poorest cottager owns more goods than the chieftains of yore. In the future, everyone will be rich."

"There are other forms of poverty, Signor. Your ledger is incomplete. What about customs, traditions, values? Should we swap these in your market, too? Poor Sicily already has pawned so much!"

"What could be more valuable than universal happiness and prosperity?"

"Pride!" I said. "Honor! Grace! These things should be preserved!"

"Like your relatives in the Cappuccini?" he sneered. "Mankind will never be happy until it frees himself from the mummery of the past."

Signor Bentham, I reminded him, was also a mummy. I had seen his remains when I visited the University of London. Bentham had willed his body to be preserved and displayed in a wooden cabinet in a gallery of the anatomical museum. During his last years, he supposedly carried the glass eyes for his skull in his coat pocket. "Unhappily," I said, "the embalmer botched the process. Your great philosopher's head shrank into a ball of *baccalá*. A wax head has been substituted, and the mummy is wheeled into meetings of the college council. I can imagine the minutes: *'Jeremy Bentham—present but not voting.'* The college has stored the skull, incidentally, because the students were using it for rugby practice."

"Well, Jos?" prodded Don Benjamin.

Signor Whitaker shrugged. "Humanity is foolish in the individual, wise in the mass. That's why markets work."

"And so the economy is a perfect engine, and we are but poor cogs."

"If you like," said Signor Whitaker.

"All engines break down," I warned.

"Not this one," he said. "Either climb aboard or be run down."

∾ "Stop!" I shouted from the balcony.

Below the Red Shirts had wheeled my carriage into the courtyard, and the corporal ordered someone to fetch an axe. I shrieked. Rage aggravated my limp, and I hobbled down the stairs, grabbed my whip, and lurched into the courtyard. The corporal stood, hands on hips, with one foot on the running board. None of the servants or field hands interfered. They stared at me then looked away, to hide their shame or delight. Regina stood under a palm, cheering and waving a red banner. Someone ran out of the tool shed, and the corporal motioned for the axe.

I cracked my whip. "You will not touch that carriage!" I said.

The corporal squinted behind his spectacles. He was barely taller than I, slight and refined, and his crest of red hair perked like a coxcomb. "You ignored the Duce's edict," he said. "You know the consequences."

"The Duce," I scoffed. "A fine democratic title."

"Sicily is a republic now, Signora," he said, "and the General its temporary dictator."

"Tell Cincinnatus to return to his goats! And you," I said, menacing with my whip, "stay away from my carriage!"

He tossed his head, and two Red Shirts seized me. I lashed one across the face. When his companions aimed their rifles, the corporal raised a hand and restrained them.

Bridling, I glared at the men. "Shoot!" I demanded. "Show yourselves for the cowards you are! Just because I'm a woman, doesn't mean I'm a dog! I won't lick your heels!"

A bluff. I was terrified. Terrified and heartbroken, since I knew it was hopeless. Everyone else had surrendered. How can you fight a volcano? Those Red Shirts flowed like lava. So many fine estates pillaged, so many beautiful wardrobes burned, so many elegant carriages confiscated. During the Palermo riots, the mobs dismembered and devoured Bourbon spies. Some they ate raw in front of the home of the American consul. Others they roasted on bonfires like boars at a Cuccagna. That is the trajectory of civilization—from monarchy, to democracy, to cannibalism.

Eyes hungry, teeth bared, the soldiers strained at the leash, but the corporal merely removed and cleaned his glasses. He spoke calmly. "You're very brave, Signora, but your courage is based on pride."

I reeled on him. "I've a right to be proud! I know who my people are! Who are yours? Where do *they* come from?"

"From Adam and Eve, Signora. Same as everyone else."

The Red Shirts laughed, and Regina giggled, hopped, and clapped.

My eyes narrowed. "Little Corporal," I sneered. "Little Bonaparte. What were you before you wore that butcher's smock? A tailor, a watchmaker?"

That was my mistake. Aroused, the corporal—eyes blazing—strode over, wrested the whip, and twisted my arm behind my back. "I was a teacher, Signora," he growled in my ear. "I taught the classics in Cuneo, before I joined the Alpine Hunters. Now I'm going to teach you a lesson in Roman history."

He grunted, and two soldiers grabbed and dragged me, kicking and screaming, to the carriage. The corporal tested the axe blade with his thumb and spoke as if lecturing to a class: "From Suetonius' *Lives of the Twelve Caesars*," he said and bowed.

"When the Emperor Claudius revived and assumed the office of censor, he confronted a patrician who owned a silver chariot with golden wheels. This man had so demoralized the Palatine with his arrogance and ostentation, had so jeopardized pedestrians in the streets with his recklessness, that he had been reported to Caesar. Claudius decided to punish him personally. He borrowed a ceremonial axe from a lictor, and, with his own palsied hands, destroyed the chariot."

He turned to me and smiled. "Garibaldi is censor of this island, Signora, and I, his tribune, will execute his orders. Long live the Republic!" And with those words, he massacred my carriage. He smashed the glass, splintered the frame, gutted the upholstery. The soldiers laughed, Regina clapped and cheered, I howled and struggled in vain. When he had finished, the corporal threw the axe on the heap and dusted his hands.

"Everybody rides or everybody walks. That is justice," he said.

And Regina cried: *"Viva Garibaldi!"* And danced on the wreck. That was the last straw. Shrieking, I broke free and lunged at the girl. She thrashed as I slapped her repeatedly. The corporal grabbed my hair and dragged me off Regina. When I scratched his face, he seized and snapped my wrists. The pain brought me to my knees.

The corporal squatted beside me, almost apologetic. "If you touch her again, I regret I must kill you. General's orders. We heard what you did to her the last time we were here. So take my advice: be more of a *nonna* and less of a *marchesa*."

He rose, wiped Regina's bloody face with the edge of his tunic, and addressed the men.

"*Andiamo!*" he said. "Our work here is done." He spat on the shattered ebony and gold. His men filed past and did the same. Furious, I staggered to my feet, soiled and bleeding. "Pedant!" I spat. "God damn you and the gaucho you serve!" The Red Shirts marched off. My wrists dangled at my sides like a broken marionette's. Stomping the dusty ground, I shouted: "*Passa Savoia! Passa Savoia!*"

The schoolmaster sang:

> *Savoia! Savoia!*
> *Si vince e poi si moia*
> *Finché l'Italia unità la sarà!*

The Red Shirts laughed.

✎Well, I suppose it *was* funny. A professed atheist calling curses down from heaven. But what good is God, if He won't damn your enemies? I remember Papà once showing me a passage in Thomas Aquinas, in which the Angelic Doctor claims that one of the most exquisite pleasures of the blessed is witnessing the torments of the damned. "If you had shown me this sooner," I said, "I might have taken my catechism more seriously." He laughed and kissed me.

The schoolmaster was killed at Milazzo, by the way. Tuna fishermen cut up his body for bait. Let it not be said that prayers go unanswered. A pity he never lived to see your world. He would have been pleased. Everybody rides, just as he would have wished. The streets are impassable, the noise is deafening, the clouds are filthy, but everybody rides. Such are the blessings of progress. Ah, humanity! God, in despair, no longer hopes we will grow wings. He is resigned to let us roll on wheels. Well, we are such ridiculous contraptions.

It reminds me of that Leopardi dialogue, "The Bet of Prometheus." At a science fair on Mount Olympus, Prometheus fails to receive a prize for inventing man. When Momus, the god of mockery, teases the loser, the outraged titan wagers he can prove his invention deserves the blue ribbon, if Momus will accompany him across the seven continents. But after witnessing cannibalism in Peru, suttee in Bombay, and a murder suicide in London, Prometheus admits defeat and pays up ...

"Very droll," I said. "Did you steal the idea from Lucan?"

"Actually," Leopardi replied, "the inspiration was a lecture I had attended in Rome. An English panegyric to progress."

"Ah yes, the new immortals: the English and their American cousins. You should have set your dialogue at a London exhibition, Contino. Dress the gods in frock coats and hoop skirts. Let's see: Bacchus could run a distillery; Minerva a factory producing bath oil made from olives; and Vulcan, dear Vulcan, could manufacture self-heating copper pots and pans."

He snickered appreciatively. "I see you're as skeptical of the new faith as the old."

"The old faith at least was aesthetically pleasing. Who can endure this religion of progress?" I asked. "God is no longer a king or a savior but a grocer."

"Who promises salvation in this life rather than the next. Well said!"

"Salvation," I grumbled. "*Puah*! What do the middle classes know of salvation, Signor? They promote education and hygiene and believe the only mortal sin is impropriety."

"To be fair," Leopardi conceded, half-heartedly, "the English standard of living—"

I snorted. He sounded too much like Signor Whitaker. "*Half* living, you mean. I've visited London, *carinu*. It was awful. Ugly furniture, insipid food. Everyone was abysmally dull. The mummies in the Cappuccini are livelier company. Better dressers, too."

Leopardi nodded. "Our liberal intellectuals are no better, Marchesa. You will find them in all the coffee-houses, solemn as priests and punctual as bankers. The New Believers, I call them. Apostles of virtue and reform, too stupid even to be unhappy. Still, couldn't Naples benefit from more furniture and food, no matter how ugly and insipid? The poverty of this city—!"

He broke off with a sigh and shook his head.

"*The poor will always be with you,*" I quoted. "The most sensible thing Christ said."

Leopardi pounded the mattress. "Pride!" he said. "Pride, pride, pride! The besetting sin of our class! Who are we to mock the poor?!"

"*Auff*! *Generoso*! Don't burst your noble heart!" He sputtered, but before the argument could escalate, I deliberately yawned. The first rule of a good salon: *Take nothing too seriously.* "Really, Contino," I purred. "Don't be dull. You're no Carbonaro, after all. Why only yesterday, Ranieri tells me, you called the *Napolitani* a shiftless, treacherous race fit for the gallows."

Leopardi blushed and averted his eyes. "I was afflicted with a headache."

I slapped my brow. "Only a headache? *Cáspita!* What will you say if you pass a stone?"

He fixed his eyes on me and said with great dignity: "Joke all you want, Marchesa, but I genuinely love Naples."

I think he meant it. Or rather, he had convinced himself he meant it. Still, Naples seems to have attracted him. "Like a planet to a star," Ranieri said. The Count was drawn to the city's spectacle and vitality, such a contrast to his own solitude and sickness. Those teeming streets! Sack-clothed friars and silken prelates, deformed beggars and shapely whores, swaggering soldiers and mincing ladies, local artists and English collectors. Why patronize the opera or wait for carnival when you could promenade down the Toledo? Here pasta sellers stirred cauldrons of macaroni, bakers tossed hot puff-pastry to urchins, money-changers rattled coins, barbers stropped razors, letter-writers composed epistles of love, hate, and business, fishmongers sold squirming eels and darting fish in buckets. And the din! The hawkers: "Chestnuts!" "Melons!" "Squid!" The wine-vendor beating his drum and smashing bottles, the fortune-teller spinning her clicking wheel, the hag calling lottery numbers, the street singer serenading Columbine, the puppeteer bawling *Orlando Innamorato.*

An inferno of bargains conducted in yells, shouts, and whistles, but this pandemonium was music to Leopardi's ears, so perhaps I shouldn't mock English expositions. Even the most refined genius, it seems, needs vulgar pleasures. Sometimes the Count would observe but not participate in the spectacle, slurping ices from the great confectioner Vito Pinto at that small café in the Largo della Caritá. Crouched alone at a corner table, his big head sunk into his high shoulders and his reddened eyes half closed, he would nod to passers-by or hum *"Te voglio bene assaie"* with the hurdy-gurdy.

At other times, he would master his shyness and brave the bustling market on the quay at Santa Lucia, to haggle over Swiss chard or to buy tickets for the lottery. He even suggested lucky numbers to the regular gamblers, who rubbed his hump for good luck. *"O ranavuottolo,"* they called him. The little toad. If a number won, the crowd would seize and toss him in a blanket until, giddy and overexcited, he laughed so hard he coughed up blood.

"By all means, Contino, love Naples, but don't trust her," I said. "She's a whore, through and through. She decks herself in jewels while her children go in rags."

"The sight wounds me," he said.

"Bind your wounds, then, and harden your heart! How else can one survive this world?"

My rebuke made him wary, which was the last thing I wanted. If he couldn't trust me, how could I wound him? So I softened my features and tone.

"Carinu," I purred, "I'm not made of stone. The first time I came to Naples, the *lazzaroni* made me weep. More

beggars than Cairo or Bombay. 'Save your tears!' my father scolded. 'Sicily needs every drop of water possible. We have plenty poor of our own.' But I quickly learned not to pity them."

"My God, why?" he asked, blanching. Such an innocent! I enjoyed shocking him.

"Because it's pointless," I said. "Poverty is no more eradicable than it is ennobling. That's what these progressives and industrialists don't understand. They think they can eliminate poverty with a cornucopia of things."

"Come now," he chided, "yield *some* points in this debate! Wouldn't the poor be better people if they owned more things?"

I smiled archly. "Why, I'm surprised at you, Contino. That doesn't follow, does it? We aristocrats have plenty of things, and are we better people? On the contrary, as you love pointing out, we are proud and vicious. Why should the poor be different?"

He wagged his head dubiously. "Perhaps," he said.

"No," I continued, "things are not a solution. On the contrary, they are a problem. All those English and American factories manufacturing cheap goods. The warehouses are packed with them. The shops are crowded with them. Soon the piazzas will be flooded with them. We will pile them higher than Vesuvius and hold history's greatest *Cuccagna*! You will have the honor of lighting the match, *carinu*. Just make sure you hold your nose."

"Did they really burn the animals alive in the old days?" he asked. "I was told that was anti-Bourbon propaganda."

"Oh no," I said. "That happened alright."

And I described the *Cuccagna* my father staged in Palermo one Corpus Christi, to honor the silver anniversary of Ferdinand and Maria Carolina. A replica of the royal palace at Caserta, forty feet high, was constructed in the cathedral square. Porters loaded the structure with furniture, dry goods, and barrels of wine. Butchers tethered and slaughtered oxen by the gates. Poulterers nailed chickens, capons, and geese to the walls. Sheep and swine were herded and penned inside. From the battlements hung effigies of dead revolutionaries, stuffed with grain, coins, and jewels. Fine fabrics and clothes dangled from the windows. Garlands of sausages and festoons of cheeses adorned the doors. The crowds gathered all day behind a troop of mounted cavalry officers. Standing on a platform before the doors of the cathedral, my father prepared to give the signal. I stood on tiptoe beside him and held my breath.

When dusk fell, Papà set off a rocket, and the cathedral bells pealed. The mob shouted, broke through a line of foot soldiers, and stormed the miniature palace. Battering the doors and scaling the walls, they began an orgy of looting. They shredded linens, stuffed pockets and knapsacks with trinkets, disemboweled livestock, tore crucified pigeons from the walls, leaving the twitching wings on the nails. Nobody noticed the hooded penitents approaching the structure with lighted torches. My father nodded, and the *Cuccagna* was set ablaze. As the fire quickly spread, screams, bleats, and squeals pierced the air. The noise and stench appalled the more sensitive, who covered their ears or retched into embroidered handkerchiefs. As the looters fled, loaded with goods, spectators applauded, soldiers fired rounds, and the fireworks exploded.

"My God," said Leopardi.

"From above," I continued, relishing his discomfort, "I had seen the entire show. I was so thrilled I squeezed my father's hand. Then a half-singed goose flew up and sought shelter in my arms. A ragamuffin, who had climbed the front of the platform with a dagger between his teeth, pursued her and grabbed her plump rear.

"'Gimme!' he growled, between clenched teeth.

"'No!' I said, gripping the bird's neck.

"We played tug of war, the goose honking piteously, until finally the boy yelled, 'Let me have her, you little bitch!'

"'You want her?' I said. 'She's yours!' And I released the bird. With a look of consternation, the boy fell to the piazza, breaking his neck and crushing the goose."

A terrible tragedy, I conceded. After all, the poor goose had done nothing wrong.

TOP: FEAST OF SANTA ROSALIA.
BOTTOM: PIAZZA VIGLIENA, PALERMO.

CHAPTER V
A Century of Progress

BREAD AND CIRCUSES, EH? DON'T presume to judge. You people are no better, with your malls and expositions. Lord, the *Cuccagnas* of democracy! All the world's a sale, and every day a feast! Enjoy the carnival while you can. Death is a permanent Lent. But at least one is spared the indignities of Vanity Fair.

God knows I bartered all my life. I had a genius for it. Why, then, did I fail in business? I could blame my partners, but that would oversimplify the case. Essentially, our values were incompatible. Mine was for the tangible. I always sought the best bargains at the Vucciria. It took a special cunning to navigate that market. I had to sail between the Scylla of roiling prices and the Charybdis of spoiling goods. Rot always bid against me, so I had to make an offer before the fish lost its iridescence, the meat attracted maggots, or the fruit turned into mush. My instinct never erred, but instinct is blind to the intangible. I was unfit for a world where prices are fixed and goods never spoil. In England, iceboxes preserve fresh chops, tins seal brine-cured ham, and bacon-faced men in Prince Albert jackets speculate on lard.

Christ warns us about casting our pearls before swine, but Christ never ran a plantation. Blight had ravaged the orchards. At first, we blamed the yellowing leaves on chlorosis. We had dealt with that before. The fruit would harden, the trees would wilt, but the groves would survive. But when the gnarl of barren branches became a tangle of witch's hair, we knew it was more serious. The veins and roots had been affected, and parasites had bored into the bark. *"A tristezza,"* Nino Tumeo pronounced. When I cut open an infested blood orange, it was like slicing into my own heart. It would take ten years, maybe more, to recover, so I accepted Don Joseph's offer. What good is a name without land?

After signing the contract, I went to confession, even though I did not believe in God. I needed to share my shame with someone, and Regina would have scoffed. I had done many terrible things in my life — rejected a mother, murdered a husband, condemned a poet — but never before had I whored myself ...

✑Ortensio Pitarresi smiled like a pimp. *"Comare,"* he said, with oily familiarity, "I knew you would come!"

He presumed too much. Born prematurely on my estate, he had become my godson by default. No one had expected the runt to live, so I agreed as a mere formality. Just long enough for the priest to sprinkle his head and mumble the words of baptism in garbled Latin. But the brat survived to spite me. Now he was the prissy and poodle-headed secretary at Ingham & Whitaker.

Ortensio offered me a chair. "Make yourself comfortable. I will fetch Don Joseph."

I sat stiffly and leaned on my gorgon-headed walking stick. The grandfather clock ticked the minutes, and my heart served as weight for the pendulum. *My God*, I thought, *is this the end of Trinàcria?* Signor Whitaker entered. The office lynx had aged well. Power had appeased his resentment, and his bearing had become dignified, even graceful. With Don Benjamin semi-retired, he ran the company. His diversification strategy had increased profits, and he had rewarded himself accordingly. He owned a handsome villa and played paterfamilias to a growing brood. After he added Spadafora to his name, everyone saluted him as Don Joseph.

"What can I do for you, Marchesa?" he asked, understandably wary. I had beaten him black and blue in the Quattro Canti. He had been so casual when we ran into each other at the Fontana della Vergogna. Having revised and expanded my epigrams, I was in town to see the printer. Seeing the crest on my portmanteau, Don Joseph said: "That would make a handsome trademark. The company is developing a new line of Marsala for the English market. Would you consider selling us the rights to your seal?"

I gaped as if he had slapped me. Don Joseph drew back, but I flew at him with my cane. The blows and shouts drew the *carabinieri*. "This man," I croaked, hoarse with outrage, quivering and pointing at Don Joseph, "this man has made an indecent proposal!"

The *carabinieri* frowned. Don Joseph tipped his hat and fled. I returned in high dudgeon to Villabate, only to find three cartloads of rotted fruit. Nino wept with his face in his hands. "Ruined!" he sobbed. "Ruined, ruined!" What choice did I have? Unless I swallowed my pride, we would lose everything; but I would make a *bedda figura*.

I looked Don Joseph in the eye and smiled. "I've finally decided to board the train."

Don Joseph looked perplexed, until he remembered our debate at Don Benjamin's villa. Then his face brightened, and he sprang from his chair, grabbed, and kissed my hands.

"You will never regret this, Marchesa! I swear!"

"But I insist on confidentiality. No one must know of this. No one."

"You may rely on our discretion," he said. "Marketing and advertising will be limited to Britain. If all goes well, and if you permit, we will expand into Australia and New —"

"Please spare me the details. This is difficult enough. How much will you offer?"

"Twenty thousand *onze*," he said, "plus five percent of all sales. On renewable terms."

I nearly swooned but controlled myself. "Thank you," I said. "I need a lot of money."

"We know, Marchesa. And to maximize your return, we are aiming for high volume. That is why the Trinàcria brand will be marketed as a —"

"As I said, Don Joseph, spare me the details."

"Then leave everything to me," he said with a bow. "Ortensio will prepare a contract."

"Soon, please. Before I change my mind."

"No regrets now. You're helping Sicily march to prosperity."

"But no one must know," I reminded him.

"The firm will be silent as the grave. We English have our own form of *omerta*."

And so it became our secret. We met at functions and smiled conspiratorially. I had joined Don Joseph's army of progress. In the rear, to be sure, but I became a great *vivandière*. Trinàcria flourished. Sales were brisk, and quarterly checks arrived at the Banco di Sicilia. Having saved the estate, I allowed myself to savor my success. Ironically, of course. The arrangement seemed a bizarre joke, but at whose expense? The Speaker of the House of Keys, on behalf of the High Court of Tynwald, wrote the firm to express admiration. Trinàcria was popular on the Isle of Man because its trademark resembled the Manx flag. "Nothing," he said, "goes better with spuds and herrin'!" I was proud and bemused to have brought sunny Sicily to foggy England. Even so, no one expected a notice from the Royal Commission. A Signor Galveston informed us Trinàcria had been nominated for a special award. Would Ingham & Whitaker send representatives to the Great Exhibition of the Works of Industry of All Nations? Curious and expectant, I sailed to London with Don Joseph in April.

The Crystal Palace occupied seventeen acres in the heart of Hyde Park, a glittering three-tiered arcade of steel and glass. Three times longer than St. Paul's Cathedral, the building combined simplicity and grandeur. To complement its numberless glass panes, the galleria was decorated in red, green, and blue, the wrought-iron columns striped with yellow. A soaring barrel roof allowed elms to loom in the central corridor, and the naves were landscaped with palms, flowers, statues, fountains, and wells. Hawks roosted in the rafters and contained the sparrows. The building was drained by miles of gutters, while the lavatories boasted flush toilets — a necessity considering the tons of tea and coffee consumed in the two refreshment courts.

According to the guidebook, the architect Joseph Paxton had drafted the building's design on blotting paper. Perhaps that explains why the vast peristyle turned me inside out. The sidewalls were too far to be reached in a single glance. Defeated, the eye moved upward along an infinite perspective and ended in a blur of blue haze. The effect reminded me of Leopardi: *My thought is drowned in immensity.* Thanks to this illusion, I could not tell whether the roof was suspended one hundred or one thousand feet above me, consisted of one vast plane or many small parallel angles. Distance was impossible to measure, for relentless sunlight bathed and flattened everything. The great hall had banished shadows, and without shadows, there can be no perspective. Dizzy, I clung to Don Joseph.

The inauguration rivaled anything at the Vatican.
Visitors packed the naves and galleries, while a restless
mob assembled outside. At noon Queen Victoria and her
husband entered the exhibition, accompanied by the
thunder of cannons, fanfares and the cheers of the crowd.
After the Archbishop of Canterbury offered a prayer, and
multiple choirs and a huge pipe organ performed Handel's
"Hallelujah," Prince Albert stepped forward and, as Chair-
man of the Royal Commission, delivered the commence-
ment address. A mutton-faced man in a gold-braided tunic,
he spoke with a heavy German accent:

> *I believe it is our duty to study and watch the time
> in which we live; and as far as possible, to add our
> mite of individual exertion to further the
> accomplishment Providence has ordained. Nobody
> who has paid any attention to the features of our
> present era will doubt for a moment that we are
> living at a period of miraculous transition, one that
> will rapidly accomplish the great end to which all
> history points — the unity of mankind ...*

I paged through a thick catalogue, stuffed with etchings
of goods and machinery.

> *Not a unity, mind you, which breaks down the
> limits and levels the peculiar characteristics of the
> different nations of the earth, but rather a unity,*

> *the result and product of those very national*
> *varieties and antagonistic qualities. The distances*
> *separating the different nations and parts of the*
> *globe are gradually vanishing before the*
> *achievements of modern invention, and we can*
> *traverse them with incredible ease ...*

Twenty-five countries and fifteen British colonies proudly displayed their wares: the Americans a McCormack reaper, the French absinthe, the Germans a rectal thermometer.

> *The great principle of the division of labor, the*
> *moving power of civilization, is being extended to*
> *all branches of science, industry and art. Whilst*
> *formerly the greatest mental energies strove at*
> *universal knowledge, and that knowledge was*
> *confined to a few, now they are directed to*
> *specialties, even to the minutest points; but the*
> *knowledge acquired becomes at once the property of*
> *the community at large ...*

Bankers nodded, bishops beamed. Petticoated philanthropists daubed their streaming eyes with black-bordered handkerchiefs. I resumed reading.

> *Whilst formerly discovery was wrapped in secrecy,*
> *the publicity of the present day causes, that no*
> *sooner is a discovery or invention made, than it is*
> *already improved upon and surpassed by competing*

> *efforts: the products of all quarters of the globe are*
> *placed at our disposal, and we have only to choose*
> *what is the cheapest and best for our purposes ...*

The emporium boasted nearly a million square feet of retail. Booths sold book covers and fountain pens, fountains and vases, bedpans and commodes, ironwork and carriages, lace shawls and cotton chemises, even factory-made heraldic chairs.

> *So man is approaching a more complete fulfillment*
> *of that great and sacred mission he must perform in*
> *this world. His reason being created after the image*
> *of God, he must use it to discover the laws by which*
> *the Almighty governs His creation, and, by making*
> *these laws his standard of action, to conquer nature*
> *to his use — himself a divine instrument. Science*
> *discovers these laws of power, motion and*
> *transformation; industry applies them to raw*
> *matter, which the earth yields us in abundance ...*

Entertainment provided a relief from browsing. For a shilling, visitors could see firework displays; a re-enactment of the bombing of Alexandria; Dr. Lynn, the electrifying conjurer, who dismembered and re-assembled himself; giant mechanical dragonflies; and the aerialist Blondin, the hero of Niagara. After a triumphant tour of Australia, New England, and South America, Blondin would perform death-defying feats on the rope. He would

run at full speed, cook an omelet in midair, ride a bicycle
blindfolded, walk on stilts, balance a chair, wave a flag.

> *Ladies and gentlemen, this exhibition provides a*
> *true test and a living picture of the point of*
> *development at which mankind has arrived in its*
> *great task, and a new starting point from which all*
> *nations will direct their further exertions in this*
> *century of progress!*

Peace hath its victories no less renowned than war, I
thought. Such rhetoric amused me. Did Britain truly believe it would usher in the millennium? But as I scanned
the hall, I understood how London could mistake itself
for the New Jerusalem. If the English were all too human,
their inventions were divine. Steam engines puffed and
whirled. An envelope-making machine spat sixty samples
a minute. An iron cage slowly lifted the plump queen
into the empyrean, from whence she tossed a bouquet.

Don Joseph left to set up the Ingham & Whitaker
booth. We would rendezvous at the awards ceremony.
Meanwhile, I attended some lectures. Herr Victor Schilt
exhibited an adding machine but was interrupted by a
stout irascible man whose face seemed carved from soap.
This was Professor Charles Babbage, a Fellow of the Royal
Society and the creator of the cowcatcher. Babbage criti-
cized the German's design because the machine lacked
a zero key. How inferior to his own Difference Engine,

a device that computed and calculated large numbers using punch cards. Countess Lovelace, Lord Byron's daughter and a gifted mathematician, had endorsed Babbage's invention. The professor praised her.

"There's more poetry in one of her logarithms," he said, "than in all of *Childe Harold.*"

"Really," I drawled.

Frederick Collier Bakewell, a Yorkshire physicist who had patented a chemical telegraph, demonstrated something called a facsimile machine. Adapting a prototype from Scotsman Alexander Bain, Bakewell had perfected a device capable of reproducing an image line-by-line. I volunteered my insignia for the demonstration.

At a transmitter, the seal was traced with varnish on tinfoil, wrapped around a cylinder, and then scanned by a conductive pen mounted to a pendulum. The cylinder rotated at a uniform rate by means of an escapement gear. At the receiver, a similar pendulum-driven stylus marked chemically treated paper with an electric current as the receiving cylinder rotated. Future telegraphs, Bakewell predicted, would provide this service; but the results disappointed me. My crest seemed cheap and faded.

"This is not fit for a soup can, Signor!"

Bakewell apologized.

Alfred Charles Hobbs promoted the Parautoptic lock, his Boston company's challenge to Britain's Bramah and Chubb, which were considered as impregnable as Gibraltar. More so, in fact, since America recently had secured the key to the Mediterranean. But the mechanical spirit never rests. If lulled into complacency in one branch of an industry, it springs up elsewhere to admonish and reproach. Behold! Like a magician, Hobbs picked his rivals' locks. Amazement and applause turned to consternation, however, when Hobbs took apart the Parautoptic and explained how it worked. A constable objected. Was it ethical to give tips to burglars?

"Thieves are very keen in their profession," Hobbs said, "and already know far more than we can teach them. And what's a thief, anyway?"

"Someone who steals more than you do," I replied.

Dr. George Merryweather, honorary curator of the Whitby Literary and Philosophical Society's Museum, spoke on the Tempest Prognosticator, or, as he described it, "An Atmospheric Electromagnetic Telegraph, Conducted by Animal Instinct." Simply put, the device was a barometer operated by leeches. For years, scientists have noted how medicinal leeches react to electrical conditions in the atmosphere, as evident in this couplet from Edward Jenner's poem *Signs of Rain*: "The leech disturbed is newly risen; Quite to the summit of his prison." The doctor's invention exploited this biological principle.

Resembling an Indian temple, the barometer comprised twelve pint bottles in a circle around and beneath a large bell. Atop the glasses were small metal tubes, which contained a piece of whalebone and a wire connecting them to small hammers positioned to strike the bell. "After securing this mousetrap contrivance," Dr. Merryweather explained, "I pour rain water into each bottle, to the height of an inch and a half and then place a leech in every bottle. As a humanitarian gesture, I arrange the bottles in a circle to prevent the leeches from feeling the affliction of solitary confinement. If a storm approaches, the leeches will crawl up the bottles, enter the tubes, and ring the bell."

"You dote on your leeches, Dottore," I observed after his talk.

"Yes," said Merryweather, "I call them my jury of philosophical councilors."

"Then I presume your human colleagues are also blood suckers?"

As Merryweather fumed, I checked my watch: quarter to four. I had a pressing appointment in the Pantheon.

❧Despite the cavernous sprawl, I easily found the port and sherry exhibit in the east wing. The commissioners had divided and categorized the floor grid according to country and product. Flushed and jovial, the judges appeared to have been sampling the entries for the past three hours. A great tom turkey in a waistcoat and pince-nez effusively greeted me.

"Trinàcria, I presume? Sir Humphrey Toper."

I smiled and curtsied. Sir Humphrey bowed and kissed my hand.

"*Piacere*, Marchesa," he said. "I served on the *Agamemnon* with Nelson and remember well the charms of Palermo."

He hooked my arm and introduced me to the beribboned judges, who told me what a wonderful thing I had done for Sicily.

"I understand you are also an authoress," Sir Humphrey said. "Would you like to include your books among the samples? You're quite welcome to sell them."

I politely declined and joined Don Joseph on the dais. Liveried ushers opened the doors and began seating the guests. The buzz grew until Sir Humphrey gaveled for silence.

"Welcome to this special session on fortified wines," he began. "Historically, England has strong ties to these products, both financial and emotional. After developing industries in the Mediterranean, we have reaped rewards more precious than profit. What would the admiral's cabin be without port? The don's study without sherry? Cold, barren cells. Today's ceremony is but small recompense for centuries of comfort and pleasure."

The audience applauded, and Sir Humphrey beamed.

"Gathered this afternoon," he said, glancing at me, "are contestants not only from Spain, Portugal, Madeira, and Malta, but also from Sicily. This heartens us! Italy, so sadly under-represented at this great exposition, deserves to take her place among free nations!"

"Hear, hear!" someone cried. Warm applause. Since when, I thought, is Sicily Italy?

"If the glow of the sun, the smile of the sky, the jocund vintage, the charm of poetry, the spell of art, the enchantment of music, the grace of manners, the pride of tradition, the pomp of state, or the skill of priestcraft, could exalt a nation, Italy would look down from on high upon this raw northern land. But no, she lies in the dust, and national calamities trample her corpse. Italy wants what England enjoys — a better inspiration than that of art, and a better guide than that of priestcraft. She has tried all the ancient creeds — art and music and learning; the cult of antiquity and the art of love — but she has shut out the gospels and capital. Let these in, and see, in a generation or two, whether Italy will wallow as she wallows now!"

"More matter, less art," I interjected. "To quote the Bard."

The audience laughed, but Sir Humphrey remained ruddy and affable.

"Indeed, *signora*, indeed. And we have weighty matter to discuss."

Sir Humphrey explained the award system: The exhibition gave three types of medals, based on intrinsic rather than relative merit. These had quite distinct criteria, and it was vital for both entrants and the public to understand these criteria clearly. The Council Medal recognized outstanding and original innovation of ideas or their application, while the Prize Medal recognized outstanding execution of ideas, whether original or not. Honorable Mention was reserved for those whose work fell short of or outside of the required standards but nonetheless possessed noteworthy merit. Corroborated by a jury of impartial experts, the judge's decisions were final and beyond appeal.

"And so let us begin. The Council Medal for *outstanding innovation* goes to Companhia Geral dos Vinhos do

Alto Douro, whose new insecticide has reduced phyllox-
era by twenty percent in Oporto's tempranillo vineyards.
A mixture of calcium arsenate and baking soda, this
powder kills pests without harming grass or livestock."

Polite claps as a shy bespectacled man rose, bobbed,
and accepted the award. Blushing like a bride, he tripped
on returning to his seat.

"The Prize Medal for *outstanding execution* goes to
Vinicola Hidalgo for its Manzanilla Pasada. Concentrated
and contemplative, this classic fino sherry is very fruity,
flavored with apples, pears, and olives, but possesses a
salty tang. Well done!"

The judges pounded the table as a mustachioed fop
in a ruffled shirt and black vest swaggeringly claimed
his prize. He invited everyone to visit the sandy vineyards
of Sanlúcar de Barrameda, "where the Guadalquivir River
kisses the sea," as his family's guests.

"And now," Sir Humphrey announced, "Honorable
Mention ..."

Don Joseph shook my shoulder. My scalp tingled.

"The judges are grateful for this category. Its flexibility
allowed us to vote our heart."

The audience stirred, intrigued.

"Technically speaking, the following product is not
a wine. Also, its modest price almost disqualified it out-
right. Excellence is rarely cheap."

Vexed and confused, I turned to Don Joseph, who
tugged his collar and fidgeted.

"But we received so many glowing testimonials from the public, the most touching from ordinary laborers who have brought a touch of refinement into their coarse lives. For this reason, Honorable Mention goes to Ingham & Whitaker for Trinàcria, England's most popular Marsala vinegar! At thruppence a gallon, it's an elegant but affordable alternative to malt!"

A cataract of applause. Stunned, I awkwardly rose. A bronze medal slid down my neck, and I bowed my head and cried. Convinced I was overwhelmed by the tribute, Sir Humphrey patted my cheek, but I staggered from shame. The medal weighed more than a dead albatross. Spectators pointed and laughed. A lobster-faced colonel, on leave from India, remarked: "These Dagos are so demmed emotional!" I kept my dignity. But when the *Times* the next morning christened me the Vinegar Marchesa, I vowed to murder Don Joseph.

‰ "Where is he?" I demanded.

"Sensibly hiding in the *baglio*," said Don Benjamin. "Please calm down, Zita."

"Not until I drink his blood! That bastard lied to me!"

"He respected your desire not to hear the truth. It's not the same thing."

"I never would have consented if I had known!"

Don Benjamin shrugged. *"Caveat emptor.* You got what you wanted."

"Did I want to be turned into vinegar?!"

"You're being ridiculous."

"Navvies sprinkle me on fish and chips! Scullions use me to boil away grease!"

"Be grateful for them. Their custom allows you to keep your villa."

"But the shame, Don Benjamin! I will never forgive him!"

"It was my idea."

I stopped and stared. *"Your* idea?"

"You needed a lot of money, and we could make more pushing cheap vinegar at high volume than selling another expensive wine."

"Your idea," I said.

"I was thinking of you."

"I'm sure you were. And what precisely, Signor, were you thinking?"

"What does it matter," he said, "so long as you have your money?"

"An excuse to spite me."

"Maybe a little. Haven't you given me cause? God, you're insufferable! When you were young, you had brains and guts and ran with the times. Now you're a stuffed dodo!"

"I'm not extinct yet, and you and your nephew will pay. I will bring you to court."

"I advise against it," Don Benjamin said. "That contract is above board. And besides, you would disgrace yourself. Right now, nobody knows about our arrangement; or if they do know, they pretend otherwise. Nothing exists outside of Sicily. But if you sue, everyone will be obliged to treat you like a laughing stock. You will ruin yourself."

"How can you speak to me like this?"

Our eyes met, and for a moment old feelings resurfaced, just as sixteen summers ago, that island arose off the coast of Sciacca. The English named it Graham Island, after the baronet who had fathered the new constitution, but the Saccensi christened it Ferdinandea, after the new king. Don Benjamin took me to see it. Sharing a telescope, we saw the water bubble and churn. Sightseers on the wharf speculated. Was this phenomenon a volcano, an atoll, or a kraken? A geologist wanted to explore the island for specimens. A major wanted to construct a new fort. The mayor wanted to launch a ferry. We eavesdropped, shook our heads, and chuckled. Suddenly, the gulls circled and cried. As Don Benjamin squeezed my hand, the island sank.

His eyes turned cold. "Because," he said, "you imputed the honor of this firm."

I ground my teeth. Men and their pig-headed pride!

"Honor," I jeered. "The *baglio* baron lectures me on honor."

Don Benjamin's eyes flashed, but he contained himself. "The word's precious to me, too. And if you sue me, I'll fight you tooth and nail."

No bluster. This was a promise, not a threat. But I could not back down.

"Then *en garde*, Signor. I will see you in court."

"As you wish," he said sternly. "But until this business is settled, I will honor our contract. Self-respect demands it."

And like a three-masted freighter, he sailed out of the office.

Ortensio Pittaresi entered, his ear obscenely flushed, presumably from having pressed it against the door. He crossed to the desk, shuffled his papers, and regarded me with a smirk.

"And they say chivalry is dead," he said.

My lawsuit destroyed me, exactly as Don Benjamin had predicted. Trinàcria was no match against bankers and lawyers. But then, neither was Garibaldi ...

∽"Ruined!" I crowed. "Tinkers unseated your noble knight!"

I rattled the newspaper in her face, ignoring the pain in my wrists. Gagged and lashed to the chair, Regina flailed her head. I laughed. Blessed be the ties that bind. The news from Aspromonte was so delicious I had to read it aloud.

"Why are you surprised?" I asked. "After he denounced the Prime Minister in Parliament and treated Sicily like a private fief, the capitalists wanted his head. Did he really think they wouldn't stop him? But no, he thought he could patch Italy like one of his filthy ponchos! *'Rome or death!'* Well, death is what he got! Death, defeat, and disgrace!"

The General had played hide and seek with the government troops in the Calabrian hills, confident, in his supremely naive way, they would avoid a confrontation at all costs, would, in fact, join him on his crazy march to Rome and unite Italy. But he no longer inspired blind adoration. He was older, grayer, stiffer, and his men were not the glorious Thousand but unwashed malcontents and pimply boys who grumbled when low supplies forced them to root for potatoes. By the time the General emerged from the pine forest near Aspromonte, a quarter of his men had deserted. Exhausted and dispirited, he was unprepared for the ambush.

The *bersaglieri* came up the slope, firing warning shots as they advanced. Not wanting to be the one to start a civil war, the General ordered his men to hold fire, but the more eager and undisciplined volunteers on the left and right flanks disobeyed and killed some government soldiers. Realizing all was lost and trying to prevent a massacre, the General strode before the center line, shouting: *"Non fate fuoco!"* As the bugler blew ceasefire, Garibaldi crumpled, clutching his left thigh, and fell to the ground. His aides laid him under a chestnut tree, and an officer lit a cigar and put it in the General's mouth.

The field surgeon removed the boot and examined him. The thigh wound was superficial, but a second bullet had lodged beneath a bone in the left foot. At the General's insistence *(More gaucho machismo!),* the surgeon probed the wound with forceps, using brandy as a disinfectant *(That must have stung, eh?),* when, without bugle call or any other warning, a government officer galloped up and, remaining in his saddle and refusing to salute, demanded unconditional surrender. *(Quite properly, too! Should have shot him on the spot!)* The General raised himself and said in a voice choked with indignation: "I've seen thirty years of warfare! A good deal more than you, young man! And let me tell you, negotiators never present themselves like this!"

What did he expect? Gallantry, manners, honor? That pup's father was a newspaper canvasser! What did he know of honor? No, the honor belonged to our Colonel Pallavicino. (Something of a coxcomb, to tell the truth, a little too effusive and with a penchant for male sentimentality, but he still belonged to one of Sicily's best families.) He arrived, dismounted, and, with his cap under his arm, approached the General, knelt, and kissed his hand. "I must perform a painful duty," he sighed. Could a newspaper canvasser have shown such tact and sensitivity? But Pallavicino realized Garibaldi was nothing more than a little boy who needed to be put to bed. The Colonel held the General's hand as the surgeon extracted the bullet. Supposedly, from ricocheting off a boulder before piercing the General's foot, the sharpshooter's ball had formed a liberty cap. Liberal propaganda, I'm sure.

"The point is," I said, folding the paper, "Garibaldi is finished!"

Regina reddened, strained at the ropes, and growled.

"No theatrics, girl! Life's not an opera, as that ponchoed tenor discovered. We can't sing our way to glory." And I swept to the piano and bawled:

Suoni la tromba, e intrepido
Io pugneró da forte
Bello affrontar la morte
Gridando: "Libertá!"

Regina didn't care for Bellini, judging from the snarls. I laughed and hammered the keys. "The opera is over," I calmly announced, "and life can return to normal. The gaucho has been stopped!" Exultant, I rushed to proclaim my joy to the world. I threw open the French doors and, despite my bad leg, pranced onto the balcony.

"The gaucho has been stopped!" I cried. "The gaucho has been—"

A sharp pain exploded in the base of my skull, and for a moment I thought a sharpshooter had killed me. My face and side went numb, and I pitched over the balcony and grabbed the balustrade. While my feet scissored in midair, the workers shouted and fetched a ladder. But my damaged wrists gave way, and I fell ten feet and lay sprawled on the courtyard. The men rushed to my shattered body. My neck was twisted, my mouth frozen in a silent scream. Nino Tumeo removed his cap, shook his head, and spat.

"What a heap!" he said.

But the real fun came later! Regina became my torturer as well as my caretaker, repaying me for every wrong I'd done. She was inventive, I'll give her that much. But, then, she had learned from a master. For national holidays, she dressed me in a red tunic, stuck a flag in my hand,

and wheeled me to local celebrations, hissing taunts in my ears whenever the crowd cheered. On anniversaries of the Thousand, she disrupted my sleep by pounding Verdi marches and revolutionary hymns: *"Garibaldi fu ferito/ fu ferito ad una gamba!"*

During Lent, she forced me to endure preachy excerpts from the *Purgatorio*. Her favorite was the story of Sapìa Salvani, a Sienese noblewoman who taunted God when she witnessed an enemy's defeat from her balcony. Supposedly, Sapìa was saved from final damnation only through the intercession of a devout comb merchant. I don't know what offended me more, Dante's awful punning (*"Sapìa I was, but not sapient"*) or his middle-class morality. What did that self-righteous Tuscan know about Purgatory? He imagined it as an exhilarating climb up a seven-story mountain, but it is nothing but paralysis.

If you want to know the truth, Regina, go to Càccamo and visit the Chiesa dell'Anime del Purgatorio, where trapped souls writhe on the stucco walls and bare skeletons are stacked like cordwood in the cellar. But what did it matter? I wasn't human anymore. I was a rag doll, a tailor's dummy. My mind scuttled on the void like a gecko on a blasted wall. Twenty years of that penance! But don't pity me. How will you die: in the throes of passion or pissing into a catheter? In the end, we are so much *baccalá*. And sometimes, years before the end. Remember, there are two deaths: the one the coroner records, and the one that matters to you. I should have died decades sooner, but at least my stroke gave me a genuine advantage.

When I finally came to the Cappuccini, the mummies marveled at how well I took to my new state. *Why, Zita!* they exclaimed. *You're so good at being dead!*

"Practice, *miei cari*. Practice," I said.

∽ "Practice, Contino," I said. "It takes practice and reason to conquer the emotions."

"Reason cannot cut out the heart, Marchesa. Believe me, I've tried."

"Why cut anything?" I said. "Why wield reason like a scalpel, when you can use it like a needle? One well-placed stick, one tiny pinprick, and you are inoculated against love."

"So now Signor Jenner has the cure for love?"

"Certainly," I said. "Love is a major source of the pox, isn't it?"

Ranieri brayed, but Leopardi moped. "Women already are immune to me," he said.

Ranieri sighed and shook his head. A common refrain, no doubt. Poets are never more tedious than when they bleat about love. Leopardi often apostrophized the Woman Who Can't Be Found. Well, he might have found her if he had bathed occasionally. Spittle and food encrusted his shirt, the collar and cuffs begrimed with sweat. When his great love Fanny Targioni was asked why she had rejected him, she spat: *"Puzzava!"* He stank. Ranieri wrinkled his nose as he arranged the bedding. He should have smothered that toad with the nearest pillow.

"Some ladies, *carinu*, don't appreciate posies of verse."

I showed my teeth and let the words sink in. I had not forgotten Trinàcria marking and shelving her lovers. He didn't hear the threat. On the contrary, my words oddly cheered him: "How can they resist such a beauty mark, Marchesa?" He chortled and caressed his hump.

I scowled and rapped my ebony walking stick on the tiled floor. The silver gorgon's head glared between my thumb and forefinger. "Refrain from such buffoonery in my presence! It's beneath your dignity as a nobleman!"

Ranieri whistled in mock horror, as only a Neapolitan can. But a smile flickered on Leopardi's thin, filmy lips. He raised a playfully scolding finger. "You should be more respectful towards hunchbacks. In your native Sicily, they are considered sacred."

Yes, those silly fairy tales Mamma used to tell. Once upon a time, there was a hunchback, Zita, a wandering woodsman. One day he met the three fates in the forest. The old women, who had been weaving for hours outside their cottage, were too tired to make a fire, so the hunchback chopped them some kindling. As a reward, the fates sliced off his hump with a cheese saw, salved his back, and hung the hump on a tree. When the hump dried, the fates made a bagpipe out of it. The woodsman played, and the old women danced. Vexed by this unwelcome memory, I sneered: "Only among peasants, Contino. Among the educated, hunchbacks are hunchbacks."

To my surprise, he laughed. Why did he indulge me? Was it because it was my birthday, or because I was an aging flirt, whose hair and clothes were twenty years out of fashion? My beauty was fading. Intimidation had replaced charm at social events, but that fierce-looking walking stick no longer diverted attention from my limp. Beneath my silks and satins grew a spider's web of varicose veins. *Yes*, I admitted, *I'm as ridiculous as he.*

Holding his sides, Leopardi said: "The educated can learn something from peasants."

"About hunchbacks?" I retorted. "Your vanity amazes me!"

"I mean," he said, keeping his composure, "about the imagination."

"The only thing peasants imagine is becoming noblemen, and *liberté, égalité, fraternité*, be damned!"

"That's very cynical."

"Also true. A form of compensation. When one can't have carriages, gowns, and *palazzi*, one dreams about them, or one invents stories in which one gets them. That's all imagination is: compensation."

"The imagination," he said, "is the primary source of human happiness."

Too vehement, I thought. *He's hiding something.*

"You don't actually believe that, do you?"

Touché! I knew he was lying. He had an infinite capacity to believe his own words. He spoke so reverently about the peasants, but I doubt he ever talked to one. His laughter was self-lacerating. I pitied his face, so vulnerable and boyish, but Trinàcria would be avenged.

"No," he confessed, "I suppose I don't. The imagination is only a chimera. But this chimera made the ancients our superiors."

"You little fraud!" I pounced. "You satirize the Golden Age, but you still believe in it! The ancients were *not* our superiors, Contino. If anything, they were far stupider."

"But also happier," Leopardi said.

"Happier?" I said. "The Greeks thought it better not to be born, and they were happier?"

"Fuller, then. More alive."

"I doubt it," I said.

"Their world was more alive. Thunder, wind, the stars spoke to them."

I yawned. "Yes, yes, yes, all well and good. But that was because they were ignorant, *carinu*. They had no science, only stories. Illusions."

"Noble illusions."

"Foolishness," I said. "Superstition. You're not advocating superstition, are you?"

I was surprised and confused. He was a philologist and an astronomer as well as a poet. His work had an austere, mathematical beauty. Did he still believe in fables?

Leopardi looked at me as if I had insulted his intelligence. "Of course not," he said. "Like you, I trust facts. But empirical evidence shows the ancients were daring, brave, and tragic — or appeared daring, brave, and tragic — because they believed the cosmos was alive. Every stone, every leaf was an enemy or a friend. Nothing was indifferent, nothing insensate."

"But that's a fiction," I said. "The cosmos isn't alive. It's a machine, an engine. It turns forever and ignores our tears. That's the truth, and we must accept it."

He winced and gritted his teeth. His kidneys again. He fought the pain and composed himself. "I know it's true, and I accept it. But, don't you see, that's what makes life so horrible!"

I fanned myself and said nothing. Why scold the dead? Still, he disappointed me: he was no match for his own intellect. He had mastered Hobbes and Locke, Hume and Descartes, but he still couldn't live with the truth. I think he wanted to stay a child. Finally, I said: "Life isn't horrible, *carinu*, only disenchanting. But it's better that way. Hope deludes."

"Yes, ultimately it's better to live without hope. When hope is gone, so is the desire to be fooled. But, dammit, we like to be fooled!" he said, and I couldn't tell if he was angry or pleased. "My God, when I think of the human race, when I think of the fairy tales we tell ourselves to convince ourselves we matter, how the gods came down expressly for our sake to walk among us, I don't know whether to laugh or to cry."

"Then you agree with me," I said: "Truth is better than fiction."

"No, Marchesa. That's the irony. Fiction heals, truth kills."

He had a point. Truth is pitiless. How did my father put it? We must be cruel to be kind. What can be crueler than those kind Capuchins? I shuddered as I remembered how they prepared poor Papà. I had insisted on watching. Cheerfully, they cut, flayed, peeled, plucked, gutted, and tanned the corpse. The tenderest friar used the sharpest knife, the most caustic acid. *To do him justice, daughter,* he said, placing my father's spleen in a jar. A novice tittered.

Yes, truth is ghastly, but is fiction better? Stories can cauterize the heart.

"Really?" I purred. "Then why do lies murder love?"

Top map: Bourbon Sicily.
Bottom map: Bourbon Palermo.

CHAPTER VI
The Scent of Broom

 WE'RE DOOMED TO TELL STORIES, aren't we? Perhaps we believe we can persuade the fates into granting us a happy ending. That is the greatest illusion. Fate denies happiness to the living and the dead so don't be ashamed when words fail you. The nun's prayer, the poet's ode, the critic's wit end here. Silence is the mother tongue, the universal language. Sooner or later, everyone will speak it. But that won't occur until the end of time.

Meanwhile, we chatter on. The living ignore us, as is their right. We're no better than the effigies they burn at festivals. Death is a universal indignity, even for kings ...

When Francis I was waked at Caserta, he looked so splendid on that flower-strewn bier. Snuggled in a braided collar, his potato face was almost handsome. The Order of San Gennaro adorned his blue tunic, and a lily-patterned sash hid his pot belly. Suddenly, the hush was shattered by a clatter from the catafalque. Because the king's body had been hastily embalmed, his right arm had fallen off! My mocking laughter infected the mourners. The honor guards barely controlled themselves, and the court ladies fled the chapel, giggling.

One squealed: "Jove thunders!"

Carnival laughter swallows us whole. Are the fates ever sorry to see us go? ...

∽ "I must go," I said brusquely. "Will you sign this or not?"

"Of course," Leopardi said. "Your birthday present."

I placed the book in his hands. He squinted at the cover, then flipped through the pages and sniffed the binding. "Which edition is this?"

"Last year's," I said.

He smiled, pleased. "I thought the Bourbons had confiscated them all."

"Sarita had one or two extra copies hidden."

"Be careful, Marchesa. You're reading subversive literature." He winked. "They say I'm a morbid atheist, you know."

"Are you surprised? You write about singing mummies and familiar spirits. What else do you expect the pious to say?"

His face grew solemn, but the pain was more like poise now. When Ranieri showed me his death mask a year later, it wore the same expression.

"They don't understand," he said. "Even when I say terrible things, I want to console. That's the only reason a writer should write: to console. Talking about death is a way of restoring life."

"Please, Contino. You sound like you're canonizing yourself."

Leopardi laughed. "And why not? It's the latest fad in Naples."

"What ever do you mean?"

"Haven't you heard? There's talk of making Queen Maria Cristina a saint."

"Already?! But she's been dead only seven months!"

"Cardinal Caracciolo is going to Rome. Apparently, the Queen's niece, the daughter of the Duke of Modena, called upon her aunt in an emergency. Her son had struck his head on a pump and suffered a concussion. The doctors said the boy would die; but the Queen's niece prayed to her aunt, and the Queen supposedly interceded for her."

The poor simpleton, I thought. *So now they are calling her a saint.*

I had met her, when she came to Palermo for the Festival of Santa Rosalia. The city had gone wild. Streets strewn with flowers, windows hung with damask, cheering children waving sparklers. You'd think the Madonna had descended to earth! She was charming, in a way, but lacked dignity. More a soubrette than a queen. Everyone was taken by her piety, except me. She reminded me too much of my mother. Still, at her request, I accompanied her when she made the pilgrimage up to Mount Pellegrino. We entered the cave where St. Rosalia supposedly had been a hermit. The Queen asked me to recount the legend. I rolled my eyes, but got on with it. Rosalia had lived here, I explained, in solitary meditation, amid the constant dripping of water. When she died, she was preserved in a layer of stalagmite, her head crowned with roses by ministering angels. The Queen's eyes widened, and she kissed my hands. She believed every word, the fool.

By the time the Queen and her ladies retired from the shrine, dusk had fallen, but the steep path down the mountain was lit with hundreds of torches. The peasants from the countryside had come out to greet her. They accompanied her down the mountain, singing hymns. Townspeople below saw the flickering procession and set out with lanterns to welcome our carriage. Maria Cristina spoke to them when we reached the foot of the mountain. She reassured them she would pray for their souls. *"What about our bellies?"* a coarse voice demanded. "Jacobin!" I spat. "Arrest that swine!" She didn't even have pride enough to be insulted. "You'll have bread, too. I promise," said the Queen. Then a young newlywed couple came forward for her blessing. Maria Cristina stepped out of the coach and embraced the bride. I was almost moved. Almost, mind you. A pity the festival ended so badly. There was an explosion in the factory where the fireworks were being prepared. At least ten men were killed.

"I'm sorry to hear it," I told Leopardi. "I think it's vulgar and disgusting."

Leopardi frowned. For the first time, he seemed genuinely angry with me. "Why?" he said. "It's a beautiful story."

"Ah ha!" I said, and tapped his sunken chest with my fan. "I knew you were a believer!"

He smiled enigmatically and shook his head, then ran his hand over the book.

"Antonio!" he called.

Ranieri entered, with his patient, ox-like face, and helped Leopardi to his desk.

"This will take some time," the Count said. "Please —excuse me." He put his sharp nose so close to the title page I thought he would use it for a pen. Reaching for the inkstand, his hand shook. It was too painful to watch, so I turned to the window.

Such a desolate landscape. All those ruins. *He must feel like the Man in the Moon*, I thought. The one comfort was the yellow flowers dotting the slopes of the volcano. Their soothing fragrance filled the room.

"Broom," I said.

"Yes," said Leopardi. "They grow on the back of that exterminating mountain, but the lava always sweeps them away."

"So many," I marveled. "Clusters and clusters of them."

"An illusion," he said. "They are solitary plants, growing far apart from each other. Solitude sweetens their scent."

"You would have made a terrible botanist, *carinu*. What would Linnaeus have said?"

Silence. The pen nib scratched the page.

"They've uncovered more graffiti at Pompeii, you know."

"Really?" Leopardi said. "Anything interesting?"

I shrugged. "Political slogans, advertisements. Someone named Frontinus hawks chariots. Everyone must have wanted one on that last day."

"Even the best chariot wouldn't have helped, I'm afraid. The streets were jammed, and the ash thicker than snow." He blew the sand off his signature and handed me the book.

"There! More graffiti from the dead."

The inscription read: *"From one hypocrite to another,*
GIACOMO LEOPARDI."

I bridled. "You call me a hypocrite, Signor?"

"We all are," he said lightly.

"This is an outrage! I will never for—"

He placed his hand on mine. The gentle touch startled
me. "Marchesa," he said, "you were right about me: I *am*
a fraud. A fraud among frauds. But it doesn't bother me
anymore. I can accept the fact that virtue—like everything else great and beautiful—is an illusion. But what
if it were a shared illusion? What if all of us believed and
wanted to be good, strove to be compassionate, generous,
high-minded, fiery: wouldn't we be happier? Wouldn't
we find our strength in each—" He broke off, embar-
rassed. Feigning indifference, he shrugged and said:
"Words. Pay no attention."

Ranieri tried salvaging the shipwrecked conversation.
"Yes, Marchesa, pay no attention to words that may have
been said in pain or jest. We deeply appreciate your patronage. It has sustained our tiny household these many
months. Your generosity—"

"Antonio!" Leopardi scolded. "Don't play the steward!
Everyone knows the Marchesa fills our pantry, but must
we shower the poor woman with artichokes? I apologize
for any misbehavior on my part, Signora. Poets shouldn't
bite the hand that feeds them, but every now and then
they should be allowed a playful nip. As a matter of self-
respect, no? Thank you for your past kindness. We hope
you will visit us in the future."

I had been waiting for this moment. "Sorry to disappoint you, Contino, but I will not visit again. Nor will I continue your stipend. You have insulted me for the last time. Trinàcria closes her account!" And I flung the squib in Leopardi's face.

Ranieri rose. "Marchesa, please! Let me explain —"

"Silence, nurse! Empty a bedpan!"

Raineri sank. If Leopardi had been a toad crushed under a cartwheel, he could not have gaped more pitifully. But my blood was up, and his weakness goaded me.

"Did you think I wouldn't find out about your bagatelle? I, who know everything that happens in Naples as well as Palermo! With my own money, you print this filthy lampoon? Well, not another *scudo* from me! Since you like to nip my hand, die in the street like a dog!"

I gathered my things. Ranieri remonstrated, but I cut him off. My face contorted with rage, I turned on Leopardi, who now seemed removed from everything. His detachment stung my pride, so I jeered: "And let me tell you a secret, Contino. Even if you hadn't insulted me, I would have canceled my patronage. I dislike your work because it is fundamentally dishonest. That's why I've lost all respect for you. You're too intelligent to believe in God, but you're still stupid enough to believe in people — and that's willful blindness, because you know better! The world consists of fools and knaves. Those who can't accept that deserve what they get."

"Oh, worse than fools and knaves, Marchesa: crabs and mice. But we're all we have."

He coughed violently. Ranieri steadied him.

"Look at you!" I said. "Rags and bones fit for the dustman! You call yourself a count but dress like a beggar! You pretend to be a boy, when you're a dying old man! I'm four years your senior, but I will outlast you, corpse! All you have are words, and words are nothing!"

His head was bowed. Ranieri massaged his shoulders.

"Yes," he murmured, "I've paid a price for my foolishness." Then he raised his eyes and smiled. "But you've paid a price for yours, Signora."

I trembled violently and tossed the book in his lap.

"Thank you for a most unpleasant afternoon. Don't expect me to come to your funeral."

"I wasn't aware I was sending invitations."

"Scribbler!" I hissed.

I lurched out of the villa, toppled into my carriage, and rapped on the ceiling with my cane. As the driver took off down the bumpy road, my wig came loose. Leopardi's laughter pursued me for miles.

❧ The same laughter echoed in my ears as I hobbled into San Vitale church at Fuorigrotta. My cane echoed on the stone floor and vaults. I hesitated and then approached the marble slab:

> TO COUNT GIACOMO LEOPARDI OF RECANATI
> PHILOLOGIST ADMIRED OUTSIDE ITALY
> CONSUMMATE WRITER
> OF PHILOSOPHY AND POETRY
> TO BE COMPARED ONLY WITH THE GREEKS

Whose Life Ended at Thirty-Nine
Made Miserable through
Continuous Illness
Erected by Antonio Ranieri
Companion for Seven Years
until the Final Hour
To His Beloved Friend
MDCCCXXXVII

To be compared only with the Greeks. What tripe, I thought. *Must we flatter the dead as well as the living?* I examined the other epitaphs on the walls and floor of the chapel: Beloved Mother, Devoted Son, Selfless Pastor. Where are all the fools and knaves? I asked. Does eternity snub them, or do they conveniently disappear when they die? What company you keep, *carinu!* I sighed and shook my head.

"I'm sorry I didn't come to your funeral, Contino," I said, clearing my throat. "But you were an arrogant puppy, and it's what you deserved. Still, I appreciated you sending me the book. That's why I've brought you these."

I placed the broom flowers in the little vase on the stone. After crossing myself (out of habit), I lit a candle. The smoke made my eyes tear.

❧Smoke, my foot ...

I never returned there. Too squalid a tomb for so beautiful a soul. But a century later, so I'm told, they removed those crooked bones and reburied them in the heights above Mergellina, near Virgil's tomb. Tell me, reverend fathers: when the dead rise again, will my little hunchback stand straight before the Judgment Seat? I doubt it. Why should God straighten what He Himself twisted? That would be admitting a lapse in the law, and no judge will do that. Not without a bribe. And besides, the dead will not rise on that Last Day. When Gabriel blows his trumpet, they will stretch, turn over, and snore in their graves. The dead enjoy being dead, my dears. We don't want to be judged or saved. We want only to be left alone ...

∞ "Leave me alone," moaned Regina.

Tiluzzo wiped the sugar crust rimming his mouth with the back of his plump hand, his fingers still sticky with the honey puffs from the Convent of the Stigmata. Even with the house plunged in mourning—the mirrors covered with black silk, the walls hung with black crepe, the windows muffled with black velvet—he devoured these sweet airy nothings. But Regina refused them. She had renounced sweets for the General's sake, she declared, because she was now his last soldier in Sicily.

The bewildered boy burst into tears. Then, smiling wanly, he offered another sweet, but she scowled and slapped his hand, grinding the honey puff into the carpet with her heel. Rage and grief shook her doll-like frame, but the fit subsided and she trudged to and sat in the huge rocker, keeping time to the sighs of imaginary widowhood. He glanced timidly, but she looked through him, past him, her waxen face, both youthful and ancient, a composed mask. Dust motes swirled in the room, and the red tunic sagged like a defeated standard. As far as his mother was concerned, there were only two in that hothouse parlor: she and the dying General.

"Toward the end, they moved his bed near the window. He asked the attendants to draw back the mosquito net so he could better see past the balcony toward the granite rocks and the sea gilded by the sun. Propped by pillows and breathing shallowly, his life ebbed as he watched the rolling waves. He caught sight of a steamship and asked if it was bound for Sicily. 'Yes, General,' they said. 'Sicily,' he sighed, and there was a beautiful smile on his face. He was thinking of us, my son. In the middle of his suffering—the heat, the pain—he was thinking of us. '*O Cinque di Maggio*,' he breathed." And she recited the rest from memory: *O Night of May Fifth, illumined with the fire of a thousand lamps with which the Almighty has adorned the Infinite, beautiful, tranquil, solemn with that solemnity which swells the heart of the generous when they set forth to liberate the enslaved.*

"But who could liberate the General from Death, Attilio? As he struggled to breathe, the muslin curtains billowed, and two finches fluttered in from the moors and sat chirping on the windowsill. They had often visited the General on his deathbed, and he had trained them to eat pumpkin seeds from his hand. When the attendants went to shoo away the birds, our Savior rebuked them. 'Leave them alone!' he commanded. 'They aren't bothering anyone! I order you always to feed them after I'm gone!' His family, the attendants were amazed. He was himself again. But it was only the last flash of strength. The command drained from his eyes. His spectacles slid down his nose. In a soft voice, the General said: 'Perhaps they are the spirits of my two baby daughters come to take me away.' His wife and little boy wept, and the finches flew off with his soul. That was how Garibaldi died, my son, and heaven will never again make such a man. He was our holy warrior. *Nostro Gesù guerriero.*"

The General, she explained, had wanted a Viking funeral on one of Caprera's rocky beaches. If only the authorities had permitted it, and if only she had been there! She would have plucked Garibaldi's heart from the flames or leapt onto the pyre with her hero. But the authorities had buried the General in a cramped cemetery, and fate had buried her alive in Sicily.

Her slender shoulders slumped and shook, and sobs tore her chest. She was howling like an animal when Ciccio burst through the door. "Jesus! What's the matter?"

"I'm all alone!" she wailed. "All alone!"

"How can you say that? I'm here, Tiluzzo's here! Christ, you're cruel!"

"My General!" she wept. "My noble warrior!"

Ciccio shook her. "He's dead, Regina! Dead! But I'm alive! And a live rat's better than a dead lion! Don't waste your love on the dead! Love me instead!"

"No!" she screamed, pummeling his barrel chest. "No! No!" He absorbed the blows until she wore herself out and rocked her in his great hairy arms.

"It's alright," he said. "The bogey man will protect you."

Pressed against his chest, she was nearly calm, until Ciccio kissed her cheek. Then she flailed and screamed: "Monster! Monster!" Ciccio kicked open the door and called the servants: "Nofrio, fetch the doctor! Gilda, boil chamomile! And you, Priest Face" — turning to the boy — "mind that mummy till you're called!" He left the room, carrying Regina. "If you don't shut up," he roared, "I'll throw you down those fucking stairs!"

Tiluzzo and I were alone. The house was in an uproar. Regina howled in her bedroom, Ciccio swore, Gilda fretted. The wheezing doctor arrived and tramped up the stairs. *Another fine specimen*, I thought. But the conservatory was strangely calm. Tiluzzo toddled to the piano and plucked out *La Sonnambula*. Even in fragments, the melancholy tune soothed me:

> *Ah, non credea mirarti*
> *Si presto estinto, o fior! ...*

Poor Amina, weeping over a faded bouquet. What did she expect, silly goose, when even people fade? And we're not like mushrooms either. Once we dry out, we dry out. Can't be revived with boiling water. How can we boast about being made in God's image, when we're not even as resilient as mushrooms? I began coughing, and Tiluzzo broke off. He dashed over and rubbed camphor on my bony chest. When I hawked, he wiped the phlegm from my mouth, then wheeled me to the open window and unbuttoned my blouse.

"Bisnunna," he lisped, *"un po' di friscu."*

Yes, I thought, closing my eyes, *a little fresh air.* Night was falling, and the air was filled with fragrance. Such a relief from the dust and hysteria of that madhouse! I leaned back in the chair as nimble and delicate fingers massaged my temples. A voice hummed Bellini in my ear.

"You'll get well, *bisnunna*," Tiluzzo whispered. "You'll see."

"Tiluzzo!" Ciccio called.

Putting a finger to his lips, the boy kissed my withered cheek and skipped out. Only when the door closed and locked behind him, did I realize my danger. *Come back, you little fool!* I wanted to scream. *I'll catch my death here!* The cicadas rattled like dry bones in the waning light, and in the conservatory the geckos emerged from behind the curtains, beneath the pictures. A tide of fragrance advanced from the courtyard, a wave of jasmine and tuberose, mimosa and bougainvillea, with just a hint of broom. The rank sweetness lapped my chest, already burning and constricted from the camphor, and I groaned with all my might: *Tiluzzo! Help!* No use. Even if I could have shouted, no one would have heard me because of Regina.

"He will come!" she shrilled. "Our Warrior Savior! He will come with a thousand red-shirted angels! The sky will split, and he'll descend to earth on a white charger! On his cloak written in gold will be the words 'Faithful and True'!" The doctor's voice, muffled and avuncular, tut-tutted. Ciccio cursed. Then Regina cried out. *Thank God!* I thought. *The needle! I was getting such a headache!* Regina's voice slowly faded: "He will return! ... The Thousand will fire their rifles! ... The dead will dance in the street! ..."

No, Regina. The dead will not dance. Eternal wallflowers, we will sit out the ages.

The tide of fragrance had reached the wheelchair. The wave unmoored me, and I seemed to float, float on its surface, until the scent filled my lungs and soaked my clothes, and I began to drown. Strangely enough, I wasn't afraid. Even as I sank, I felt lighter than a cork. The scent of broom became stronger. Blacking out, I remembered a line from Leopardi, unread for fifty years: *"To be ship-wrecked in such a sea is sweet."*

❧ That's my story. No more reliable than yours, but at least I don't pretend to tell the truth. When it comes to the past, we are all tailors, forever altering for the most flattering fit. And even if we could tell the naked truth, who would listen? History, after all, is the trick the living play on the dead. People are not interested in the past, only the uses they can make of the past.

Take my distinguished visitor, the great impresario: a duke, no less, from one of Italy's oldest and most illustrious families. (If I told you his name, you wouldn't believe me.) He wants to create an epic about the golden age, and God help those who stand in his way. Palermo is in ruins and gangsters duel for scraps, but this glorified window dresser is convinced he can resurrect the past.

If it was simply a matter of will, he might succeed. Lean, imperious, and well-groomed, his tailored suit perfectly molded to his springy frame, he is a field marshal commanding an army of flunkies; but he will never recapture the past. He might as well catch the wind in a net. I would admire him more if he didn't ride a hobby horse.

"I am determined to achieve authenticity!" he says.

Authenticity? In Sicily? Good luck, *carinu*!

I hear the genius has cast an American actor as a Sicilian prince. When I was alive, that would have outraged me. Now that I'm dead, it amuses me. Only the eternal has the right to perfect seriousness, and that category does not include gods and heroes. Nothing lasts forever except the fates, those immortal gossips and scolds. They don't give a damn about us, but they won't leave us in peace either. Sounds exactly like family.

On the eve of my mother's departure, I kept to my bed and played sick. But I was so distressed about her going to the convent that I ran a real fever. When Mamma came to nurse me, I refused to look at her. She stroked my hair and sang a nursery rhyme. If a fairy descended from the sky, she could not match your splendor, darling beauty, in this bed of roses and flowers.

I slapped her hand.

"Zita, please. We may never see each other again."

"Who cares? It's what you want, isn't it?"

"No," she said, "it's what you want. Otherwise I would stay."

"Go then!" I said. "I've already left you!"

"You will never leave me," she said, "any more than you will leave Sicily."

"Yes, I will! I'll go to England, America!"

She smiled and soothed my brow. "You will never leave. No one does. Trinàcria is our mother and always calls us home. Leave me, she says, but you will return. Hate me all you want. You will love me yet. Because by magic, I make myself adored."

She took me in her arms. I struggled and squirmed, but she rocked me and crooned a lullaby. Slowly, slowly, I drifted away.

> *Vò, vò, vò,*
> *Dormi bedda e fa' la vò.*
> *Vò, vò, vò,*
> *Dormi bedda e fa' la vò ...*

From the terrace came the sound of waves ...

19TH CENTURY FRESCO FROM
THE NORMAN PALACE, PALERMO.

EPILOGUE
The Conquering Fly

"MY SWEETHEART," SAID THE director. With an ironic flourish, he introduced a stunted harpy in a voluminous gown. Her mantilla was as rotted as the face behind the beaded veil. The assistant designer grimaced. After a frantic search, she finally had caught up with him in the Capuchin catacombs. She blinked in the murky light.

"Who's she?" the young woman asked. Heat had wilted the bouffant hairdo, and the aviator glasses were too bulky for her Norman helmet nose.

"Our hostess," the director said. "We're renting her villa."

"A real witch," observed the assistant designer.

"Called herself Trinàcria," the director said. "Don't ask me why."

"Well," she said, whipping out pad and pencil. "Any decisions?"

The Maestro placed his hands on his hips, scanned the mummies, and jutted his chin. "That one, that one, and that one!" he pointed. "I want sketches by this afternoon!"

"What about Trinàcria?" she asked, tossing her head.

"Not authentic enough," the director replied.

The Capuchin guide, who had chewed gum through-
out this exchange, objected: *"Eccellenza*, this is a real
marchesa!"

"And I'm a real duke," the director sniffed, "so I out-
rank her."

He turned on his heels and left. The guide gazed at
Trinàcria and crossed himself.

&Authenticity was the director's lodestar, and he com-
mitted every atrocity to achieve it. He raided jewelry
shops for antique pendants and earrings. He rummaged
dumps for ancient upholstery. He scoured palazzi for
period furniture, paintings, and bric-a-brac. If an owner
refused entrance, the director would return at night with
hired punks and burgle the premises. The studio tolerated these methods because they trimmed a bloating
budget. Admiring the stockpile of junk, the publicist said:
"You would have made one hell of an auctioneer."

The chain-smoking Maestro flashed his barracuda
smile. On bad days, he went though six packs of Marlboros
and spat in a bronze cuspidor. This was a bad day.
Enveloped in an acrid blue cloud, he resembled some
mocking idol.

"Thank you, Gavin," he growled. "I know you meant
that as a compliment."

As the weeks proceeded, the smoke thickened. Always
a stickler for details, the Maestro bullied his crew. He
forced the costume designer to dye the soldiers' tunics
twenty times before he approved the right shade of Gari-

baldi red. He pressured the leading lady to keep an old embroidered handkerchief tucked into her purse, even though the linen never appeared on camera and smelled musty. When the Prince's bedroom appeared stagy, he rebuked the prop men and — with his own manicured hands — stuffed a horsehair mattress.

"Reality is lumpy!" he said.

The Sicilian landscape was less malleable. Every location shoot, the cinematographer complained, was a game of Russian roulette. A small earthquake had raised and warped the piazza at Santa Margherita Belice, distorting the proportions of the Baroque buildings and ruining the sight lines for the cameras. The volcanic springs at Macalube seemed more promising and suggestive. With its methane bubbles and brackish mud, the lunar landscape resembled the burning plains of the Inferno. But the sulfur fumes, they discovered, had discolored the filters and washed out the images. The southwest trek to Palma di Montechiaro was worse. The refinery fumes burned their throats and lungs, and the sun broiled the canisters and melted some film. The crew endured heat stroke, horse flies, and boiling sewage in open ditches to capture a dusty caravan trudging across a seared wasteland. The horses and extras shimmered in the haze.

"Bravo!" the Maestro barked through his megaphone. "Exactly the effect I wanted!"

The relieved crew applauded. The director had promised that this would be the last take. Elated, he invited everyone to the wrap party at the Hotel des Palmes. The former palazzo of Benjamin Ingham, the British Marsala king, the Palmes was a shrine to *fin de siècle* Palermo. Its hothouse atmosphere had inspired Wagner to complete *Parsifal* in ten weeks, despite nasty complaints about the bill. Here the Maestro, a passionate Wagnerite, held court amid antique chandeliers, marble pillars, and Art Nouveau murals. The mayor and his retinue attended the reception, along with the most prominent members of Circolo Bellini. Everyone seemed pleased, except a sheepish delegation from Ciminna, the small mountain town thirty miles from Palermo that had served as an ancestral fief in the film. Dressed in its Sunday best, the group presented a handwritten petition to a bewildered studio representative.

The *comune di* Ciminna, *provincia di* Palermo, respect-fully asked 20th Century Fox to rebuild its set in the mu-nicipal square. Apparently, the American tourists no longer wanted to see Ciminna's authentic Greek ruins. Instead, they wanted to pose in front of an imaginary Sicilian prince's fake palazzo and collect autographs. In exchange for this favor, the Ciminnesi pledged to offer daily masses at the Chiesa Madre di Santa Maria Mad-dalena for the film's future success and the studio's con-tinued prosperity. As a parting gift, the delegates gave the Maestro a miniature reproduction of *Our Lady of Good Counsel*. The original, they proudly noted, had been painted by Cimmina's native son, Pasquale Sarullo.

≈Three days later, at a midnight editing session at Villa Spinelli, the director chuckled over this incident as he viewed the rushes from Palma di Montechiaro. The composition was perfect. This could be the film's most striking sequence. Slowly, a shadow crossed the screen near the center. The director reversed and froze the film.

A fly had crawled over the lens during the shoot! Regarding the director, it wrung its front legs, as if craving pardon. The veins in the director's temples swelled and throbbed. He yanked the reel out of the projector and flung it against the wall. Thirty thousand dollars down the toilet because of a fucking fly!

He swore, stomped and then shrugged and lit another Marlboro. What the hell. Let it stay. The critics would mistake it for symbolism. Self-assertion, he mused, is ultimately useless. No point in strutting around and sticking one's bony finger in the world's chest and bellowing: "Do you know who I am?" Not when your flesh sags. On the set, the Maestro had pontificated about how hard stars used to work under the old studio system and reproached the young lead, his lover, for having everything handed to him. The actor retorted: "You don't think it's hard work servicing *you* every night?"

The crew laughed. Fine thanks for giving that prick his own trailer. What was he before the director had discovered him? A ski instructor from the Dolomites! But because he was the spitting image of Wagner's young patron, Ludwig II of Bavaria, the Maestro degraded himself. *Liebestod*, he joked. It is easier to command a film crew than to govern one's passions.

The director poured himself a shot glass of Averna and wandered onto the terrace, where his lover slept on a deck chair. The director gazed at him tenderly. With his arms behind his head and his full crotch, he resembled that prone telamon in the Valle dei Tempi. Lucky bastard. People fall into two categories, he brooded, the young and the dead. Youth is immortality.

The director surrendered himself to the night. Despite the lights from Palermo, Venus glowed and the mimosa was intoxicating. The director dragged his cigarette, sighed, and sipped his cordial. Life can be so beautiful, when we do not make demands. After all, mere mortals cannot challenge the gods — or studio executives.

Hollywood had set ironclad terms for the New York premiere. To allow suburbanites to catch the last trains to Greenwich and Westchester, the director needed to trim twenty minutes from his epic. Skip the historical detail. Publicity could provide any necessary background. Gavin had shown him an ad: "A stunning visualization! Nostalgia very similar to *Gone with the Wind!*" Since Americans hated subtitles, postproduction would dub the film. The leading man insisted on doing his own lip-syncing. The director winced. The American star sounded like a Bronx cabby, not a Sicilian prince. But this was nothing compared to what would happen to the Italians. As their lips shaped large Sicilian vowels, the soundtrack would spatter pellets of English. The actors would look like hippos catching peanuts, and the audience would smirk.

Indignation wrecked the director's serenity. He kicked the chair and woke his Ganymede. "You little shit!" he roared.

Hidden in a cypress, a solitary crow mocked his rage.

CATACOMBS OF THE CAPUCHINS, PALERMO.

Afterword

Medusa's Laughter

Like Sicily, *Trinàcria* has had a fascinating history. Beginning as part of another novel, this material contributed to that manuscript's string of rejections. Nobody, agents and editors declared, wanted to read about a Sicilian marchesa, even a dead one, unless she had written a cookbook. Granted, Donna Zita made a mean pasta Bellini, but she was no Anna Tasca Lanza. Unlike that other culinary marchesa, she had never started a cooking school at Regaleali or served as a consultant for Wegmans Food Markets, Inc.'s Italian Classics line. I decided to get practical.

"That's it!" I announced. "I'm cutting the Marchesa!"

My wife, a student of Jungian psychology, then rereading Jane Caputi's *Gossips, Gorgons, and Crones*, warned against this decision. Trinàcria, she reminded me, represented the chthonic female energy of pagan Sicily. Did I really want to mess with that? I told her not to be so superstitious. I was the Sicilian, not she. Unless I played ball, I would never get a contract.

My wife shrugged. "It's your funeral," she said.

It nearly was. Shortly after shelving the Marchesa, I was stricken with viral meningitis. For three months, my brain was on fire. I dreamt a jellyfish swam in my skull and stung me. When I described this to my mother, she exclaimed: *"A medusa!"*

Medusa, I learned, is the Sicilian word for jellyfish. Clearly, I had pissed off the Furies and vowed to make amends.

After a long convalescence, marked by chronic migraines, I restored, revised, and expanded Trinàcria's story until it became this book. I hope the results please her as much as they please me. After seven years together, we have reached an understanding. As Hélène Cixous observes, you must look directly at the Medusa to see her clearly—and then she is not deadly. She is beautiful, and she is laughing.

Partners and Sponsors

Without networking and marketing, however, I never would have found a press. Fortunately, I have had more helpful business partners than Donna Zita.

Frank Polizzi, editor of *Feile-Festa: The Literary Arts Journal of the Mediterranean Celtic Association*, was the first to believe in this project. He not only published an excerpt from the book but also encouraged me to submit the entire manuscript to Michael Mirolla, editor-in-chief at Guernica Editions, who immediately recognized its merit.

Because Guernica's funding from the Government of Ontario does not extend to non-Canadian authors, Michael suggested I seek a sponsor.

Debra Santangelo, founder and president of Sicilian Connections, provided a list of contacts and introduced me to consultant Roberto Ragone, whose professional motto is "Transforming Vision to Value." Former executive director of New York's Lower East Side Business Improvement District, Roberto served as marketing director for the Ciao America Film Project and as president and publicist for FIERI International, an organization of college students and young professionals interested in celebrating and promoting Italian culture.

One former FIERI colleague, Louis Calvelli, was now the executive director of the Italian Cultural Foundation at Casa Belvedere. For institutional reasons, Louis found the novel timely. Last year, Casa Belvedere capped its commemoration of the Sesquicentennial of the Risorgimento with a public debate on Italian Unification. Moderated by Cavaliere Vincenzo Marra, this lively exchange between Pino Aprile, author of *Terroni* (Milan: Piemme 2010), and Lorenzo del Boca, author of *Polentoni* (Milan: Piemme 2011) touched upon the often painful historical and political issues discussed in *Trinàcria*. Since this happy coincidence seemed like fate, *la forza del destino*, Louis agreed to sponsor my novel.

To pay for the book's editing, production, and distribution, Louis and Roberto organized an online campaign on Indiegogo and held a live fundraising event at Umberto's

Clam House in New York's Little Italy. Between August 15 and December 13, 2012, we raised nearly $8,000. Over 150 individuals, organizations, and businesses contributed to our cause. The following gave $250 or more in funds or in-kind gifts: Paul Ahlers (National Public Radio), *Best of Sicily Magazine*, the Chechile Family (Caly Services: Janitorial and Restaurant Supplies), Maria Glockner (JPMorgan Chase), the Mediterranean Celtic Cultural Association, Mark E. Miller (Miller Manhattan Property Group), Kameron Mohammed (Twangdillo), New York City's Sicilian Food, Wine & Travel Group, the Pallante Center for Italian Research, Sicilian Connections, the Sicilian Film Festival, Umberto's Clam House, and the Villabate-Alba Pasticerria and Bakery. Sicilian sculptor Emanuele Viscuso donated an original statue entitled *Music Tower*, part of a series called "Studies About Compenetration of Corporeal Substances," and the Alaimo family prepared a platter of *ossi di morti*, Sicilian almond cookies resembling human bones, for our November reception.

In gratitude for its help, all royalties will benefit Casa Belvedere. By reading this book, you will support the foundation's mission. Housed in an Italianate villa with a view of the Verrazano Bridge, Casa Belvedere hosts Italian language, culinary, art, and music classes, as well as galas, fashion shows, wine tastings, exhibits, and symposiums focused on Italian themes. These events generate cultural capital within the Italian American community.

Acknowledgements

Trinàcria blends historical fact, family legend, and imaginative speculation. My maternal ancestors were indeed petty Spanish aristocrats who settled in Bagheria in the early 18th century. My great grandfather, Don Antonio Coffaro of Villabate, really supplied Garibaldi with food and ammo before the siege of Palermo and sold citrus to Ingham & Whitaker.

Trinàcria herself is a based on two historical figures: **Antonia Vassallo** (1774-1815), Princess of Bellaprima and Baroness of San Bartolomeo, the formidable daughter-in-law of the historian Francesco Maria Emanuele e Gaetani, Marquis of Villabianca, whose 25-volume *Palmeritan Diary* remains a classic of Sicilian literature; and **Alessandra Spadafora** (1778-1851), Duchess of Santa Rosalia, Benjamin Ingham's mistress and common-law wife, who briefly appears in the novel. Otherwise, all private characters and events are fictitious but are informed by and play against actual public events.

For the latter, I consulted the following books: Harold Acton's *The Bourbons of Naples* (London: Methuen, 1955) and *The Last Bourbons of Naples* (London: Methuen, 1960); Christopher Duggan's *The Force of Destiny: A History of Italy Since 1796* (New York: Houghton Mifflin Harcourt, 2008); David Gilmour's *The Pursuit of Italy: A History of a Land, Its Regions, and Their Peoples* (New York: Farrar, Straus and Giroux, 2011); Christopher Hibbert's *Garibaldi and His Enemies* (London: Longmans, 1965); George W. Martin's *Verdi: His Music, Life, and Times* (New York: Macmillan, 1965); Iris Origo's *Leopardi, A Study in Solitude* (London: Hamish Hamilton, 1953); Lucy Riall's *Garibaldi: The Invention of a Hero* (New Haven, CT: Yale University Press, 2008); Mary Taylor Simeti's *Pomp and Sustenance: Twenty-Five Centuries of Sicilian Food* (New York: Knopf, 1989); Denis Mack Smith's *Garibaldi* (Englewood Cliffs, NJ: Prentice-Hall, 1972); George Macauley Trevelyan's *Garibaldi and the Thousand: May 1860* (London: Longmans, 1903): Raleigh Trevelyan, *Princes Under the Volcano* (New York; William Morrow, 1973); and Herbert Weinstock's *Vincenzo Bellini: His Life and Operas* (New York: Knopf, 1971)

Many people made this novel possible. Friends and colleagues Barbara Adams, Lin Betancourt, Tom Brooks, Cory Brown, Peter D'Epiro, Vincent Di Girolamo, Emanuel di Pasquale, Cindy French, Linda Godfrey, Eleanor Henderson, Liz Holmes, Eric Machan Howd, Edward Hower, Lynn Hyde, Tom Kerr, Joni Landau, Katharyn Howd Machan, Jeanne Mackin, Bridget Meeds, Jim and Hildy Mica, Jerry Mirskin, Amy Monticello, Giovanni Morreale, John Napoli, Mary Beth O'Connor, Wade Pikren, Steve Poleskie, Shona Ramaya, Catherine Rankovic, Tiziana Rinaldi, Laurie Roe, Alessandro Russell, Eileen Schell, Patricia Spencer, Jim Stafford, Catherine Taylor, Jason Tucker, Fred Wilcox, and Ellen Zaslaw provided feedback, resources, and encouragement, while administrators Howard Erlich, Leslie Lewis, Marian Mesrobian MacCurdy, Diane McPherson, Sally Parr, and

Jack Wang granted me the sabbatical leave and reassigned time necessary to complete the actual manuscript. My parents Philip and Maria and my sister Maria Teresa sustained me through illness and disappointment. I remain most grateful, however, to my wife Sharon Elizabeth Ahlers, to whom this book is dedicated, because she loves and understands Trinàcria, both the woman and the island. I consider her an honorary Sicilian.

JULY 15, 2013
The Festival of Santa Rosalia
Ithaca, New York

ANCESTRAL BUST FROM
COURTYARD OF VILLA PALAGONIA.

About the Author

Anthony Di Renzo, a fugitive from advertising, teaches writing at Ithaca College and has published in such journals as *Alimentum*, *Il Caffé*, *Essays & Fictions*, *Feile-Festa*, *The Normal School*, *River Styx*, and *Voices in Italian Americana*. His latest book, *Bitter Greens: Essays on Food, Politics, and Ethnicity from the Imperial Kitchen* (State University of New York Press, 2010) received strong reviews, most recently in *Gastonomica: The Journal of Food and Culture*. Descended from Spanish nobility, who settled in Bagheria in the early 18th century, he lives near the West End, Ithaca, New York's former Italian neighborhood, "an Old World man in a New Age town." *Trinàcria* is his first published novel.

Praise for *Trinàcria*

"History," T.S. Eliot observed, "has many cunning passages, contrived corridors." Anthony Di Renzo's novella *Trinàcria: A Tale of Bourbon Sicily* demonstrates how cunningly we all contrive to find in history only the lessons we want to. The book's narrator, to our initial surprise, is the mummified corpse of Zita Valanguerra Spinelli, Marchesa of Scalea (1794-1882), who had adopted the *nom de plume* of Trinàcria, an ancient name for Sicily. But soon the voice of this long-dead wit and *salonnière* — arrogant, erudite, and vengeful — grows as familiar to us as the thousand little lies we tell ourselves each day.

Donna Zita represents Di Renzo's spirited rejoinder to Giuseppe Tomasi di Lampedusa's classic novel *Il Gattopardo* (*The Leopard*), a nostalgic portrayal of old aristocratic Sicily and its privileged world, swept away by Garibaldi's conquest. Less objective than Lampedusa's Prince Fabrizio Corbera, Marchesa Spinelli blames the commercial and materialistic forces unleashed by Sicily's unification with the new kingdom of Italy for ushering in a vapid culture in which the presiding deity is money. But more "things" will never make people better: "We aristocrats have plenty of things," Donna Zita remarks, "and we are proud and vicious."

Di Renzo's writing is vivid and brimful of sardonic humor. He specializes in crisp evocations of outdoor scenes, such as the bustling streets of Naples or the unforgettably cruel festival of the *Cuccagna*; but the main attraction is the *marchesa* herself, a force of nature as powerful and inexorable as the Sicilian sun in July.

—Peter D'Epiro and
Mary Desmond Pinkowish, authors of
Sprezzatura: 50 Ways Italian Genius Shaped the World

"The past never dies," says Zita Valanguerra Spinelli, Marchesa of Scalea, the narrator and protagonist of *Trinàcria: A Tale of Bourbon Sicily*. Neither does the eternal appeal of Sicily. The Italian American writer Anthony Di Renzo has breathed new life into the glorious tradition of the Sicilian historical novel.

This fascinating book dialogues with literature, cinema, and the figurative arts. Di Renzo not only evokes the history of the Bourbons and the Risorgimento but also captures Sicily's aura as a "paper island," an imaginative world created by Italy's most important modern writers. His novel will remind readers of De Roberto's *The Viceroys* and Tomasi di Lampedusa's *The Leopard*, two different and perhaps even opposite works. The first seems to have inspired Di Renzo's love for the surreal and grotesque, the second his lyricism and elegiac melancholy.

Donna Zita is a fascinating character. She is romantic and enlightened, rebellious and ambitious, beautiful and mysterious. Her nickname Trinàcria, one of Sicily's most ancient names, shows her complete identification with this paradoxical island: wild but cultured, timeless but ephemeral, sparkling but bleak. For Zita, as for Sicily, the present is transient, while the past is eternal. Sicily here is simultaneously myth and reality. While the novel's historical data is accurate and authentic, this book appeals to the eye more than the mind. From the opening scene in which a Hollywood crew prepares to shoot an epic about Garibaldi's Thousand in Palermo, the reader is carried away by a montage of beautiful images. Through sheer witchcraft, Anthony Di Renzo recreates the timeless spell of the Medusa.

— Margherita Ganeri, author of
The Italian Historical Novel

A triumph of wit and eloquence, Anthony Di Renzo's *Trinàcria: A Tale of Bourbon Sicily* displays a thorough knowledge of Italian culture, weaving fascinating historical material with astute commentaries about Italian life, ancient and modern. Di Renzo creates unforgettable scenes sometimes operatic in their intensity. His confident, beguiling style will remind readers of Giuseppe Tomasi di Lampedusa's in *The Leopard* and of Salman Rushdie's at his very best. Like these authors, Di Renzo adroitly dips in and out of magical realism, but never lets technique interfere with fast plotting and vivid characterization. The novel's brilliant, bedraggled narrator, the Marchesa of Scalea (nicknamed Trinàcria, after the three-legged symbol of Sicily), is always lively, even when speaking from her tomb, full of wisdom, caustic humor and eccentric charm. Her tragicomic story makes *Trinàcria* an enormously satisfying historical novel.

—Edward Hower, author of
The New Life Hotel and *Storms of May*

Anthony Di Renzo's *Trinàcria* peels away layers of 19th-century Sicilian history in a way that academic and popular studies of this period cannot. The novel provides an intimate perspective on sweeping public events. Di Renzo tells the story of Zita Valanguerra Spinelli, Marchesa of Scalea, who is a composite of two historical figures: Antonia Vassallo, Princess of Bellaprima, and Alessandra Spadafora, Duchess of Santa Rosalia. During her long life, Donna Zita meets kings and queens, great composers, poets, and foreign entrepreneurs seeking to make their fortunes off her island's bounty. Di Renzo's sardonic depiction of the Marchesa's deeply felt cynicism often kicks the modern reader in the gut: the brutality of husbands toward wives; the cruelty of fathers toward children; the impact of a woman's revenge and of her unyielding, unforgiving pride; above all, the lost promise of Italy's Unification to Sicilians. This finely crafted novel glitters with polished metaphors and sparking epigrams. It is a marvelous work in the tradition of Dacia Maraini's *The Silent Duchess*.

—John Keahey, author of *Seeking Sicily*

What a great read this novel is, better than a trip to Sicily! Full of shock and delight, *Trinàcria* forms a fascinating epic about Bourbon Palermo on the eve of disaster. In the book's title character, the Marchesa of Scalea, Anthony Di Renzo creates a woman who demonstrates the folly and passion of living life defiantly on the brink. Few writers are better at showing the intimate, sometimes comic connections between the past and the present, between the old world and the new. If you love wit and discovery, you will enjoy *Trinàcria: A Tale of Bourbon Sicily.*

—**Jeanne Mackin, author of**
The Sweet By and By and *Dreams of Empire*

Trinàcria: A Tale of Bourbon Sicily is a completely original look at a long-maligned and misunderstood island—a part of and yet always apart from the modern political construct of Italy. In a work rich with history, Anthony Di Renzo takes the reader into Sicily's pre-unification past by having the mummified dead of Palermo's Capuchin catacombs confront a film crew from Italy's *dolce vita* era. This fascinating metaphysical and psychological landscape is replete with Red Shirts, petty nobility, studio hacks, and two centuries of bitter Sicilian wisdom. "We all have skeletons in the closet," says the Marchesa of Scalea, the novel's narrator and protagonist. "If they must rattle, they may as well dance." And dance they do in a macabre but spirited tarantella.

—**Paul Paolicelli, author of**
Dances with Luigi and *Under the Southern Sun*

Most historical fiction paints the past in flattering oils. *Trinàcria: A Tale of Bourbon Sicily* is etched in acid. Goya could have created this novel's caustic characters, particularly its protagonist and narrator, Zita Valanguerra Spinelli, the baleful Marchesa of Scalea, whose crest is modeled after the three-legged gorgon of Sicily. Donna Zita recounts her life from a crypt in Palermo's Capuchin Catacombs. Outrage over lost privilege has given her a posthumous case of acid reflux. But as the Marchesa relives past violations — her land scorched to dust by the pitiless Sicilian sun; her carriage hacked to pieces by Garibaldi's Red Shits; her crest and *nom de plume* Trinàcria, the ancient name of Sicily, turned into a label for cheap, mass-produced vinegar — readers learn to sympathize with this spiteful banshee.

Anthony Di Renzo's masterful, richly textured and layered narrative never hesitates to challenge its own discourse of storytelling, to question the ways craft transforms history into fiction. But it also poses an ethical challenge. Like the Marchesa, the author confronts our complacency and demands that we examine our own vanities, political hubris, and fragility. Will we take responsibility for our individual and collective histories or float into oblivion, thinking life was all a trick? This spellbinding narrative leaves us with no answers, only the lingering scent of broom.

—**Shona Ramaya, author of**
Flute, Beloved Mother, Queen of Night and
Operation Monsoon

Printed in July 2013
by Gauvin Press,
Gatineau, Québec